THE BLACK LAKE

THE
BLACK LAKE

Hella S. Haasse

Translated from the Dutch
by Ina Rilke

Portobello
BOOKS

Published by Portobello Books 2012

Portobello Books
12 Addison Avenue
London
W11 4QR

First published in Dutch in 1948 as *Oeroeg*
by the Collectieve Propaganda van het Nederlandse Boek
as the Book Week gift, subsequently published by
Querido, Amsterdam, Netherlands.

The publishers gratefully acknowledge the support of
the Dutch Foundation for Literature.

N ederlands
letterenfonds
dutch foundation
for literature

A CIP catalogue record is available
from the British Library

2 4 6 8 9 7 5 3 1

ISBN 978 1 84627 323 0

Text designed and typeset in Sabon by Patty Rennie

Printed in Italy by Grafica Veneta S.p.A.

THE BLACK LAKE

Oeroeg was my friend. When I think back on my childhood and adolescence, an image of Oeroeg invariably rises before my eyes, as though my memory were one of those magic pictures we used to buy, three for ten cents: yellowish, shiny little cards coated with dried glue, which you had to scratch with a pencil to reveal the image underneath. That is how Oeroeg comes back to me when I delve into the past. The setting may vary, depending on how long ago the period I am recalling is, but Oeroeg never fails to appear, be it in the overgrown garden at Kebon Djati or on the reddish-brown muddy paths along the *sawahs* in the Preanger highlands, in the hot carriages of the little train we took to primary school each day in Soekaboemi, or later, at the boarding-house when we were both at school in Batavia. Oeroeg and me, playing and tracking in the wilderness; Oeroeg and me, hunched over our homework, our stamp collections and forbidden books; Oeroeg and me, ever together, during each and every stage of our development from child to young man. I think it is fair to say that Oeroeg is imprinted in my being like a brand, a seal – now more than ever, since every form of communication has been banished to the past. I do not know why I feel the need to take stock of my relationship with Oeroeg and of all the things he meant to me, and still means. It may be something to do with what I felt was his inescapable, unfathomable otherness, that secret of spirit and blood which posed no problems in childhood and youth, but which now seems all the more confounding.

Oeroeg was the eldest son of my father's *mandoer*, and like me was born at Kebon Djati, the estate managed by my father. We were only a few weeks apart in age. My mother was very fond of Oeroeg's mother. As a young woman fresh from Holland and deprived of contact with other members of her sex and race at the remote plantation, my mother must have found sympathy and devotion in the gentle, cheerful Sidris. Their bond was strengthened by the fact that they were both pregnant for the first time. With my father away on his inspection rounds of the tea gardens or in his office at the factory, my mother and Sidris would pass the long hours of the day sitting on the back veranda with their sewing. They would share confidences in a gentle game of questions and answers, recounting their experiences, fears and desires, the countless changes in mood and emotion that only find response from woman to woman. They saw things in different ways and had a poor command of each other's language, but beneath the peignoir and the sarong burgeoned the same miracle. So it was not surprising that those hours of intimacy continued after Oeroeg and I were born, with me in my flounced rattan cradle beside my mother's chair and Oeroeg in the batik *slendang* on Sidris's back.

The earliest image I can recall shows me the two women sitting between the marble columns of the back veranda surrounded by piles of white laundry for mending, and Oeroeg and me in identical striped playsuits, on all fours by the potted ferns flanking the veranda steps. There were splashes of dazzling red, yellow and orange shifting in the breeze – which in later years I knew to be the closely planted cannas in the back garden. Oeroeg and

I scratched about in the gravel in search of translucent pebbles, which the natives sometimes burnished to resemble semi-precious stones. The air was abuzz with insects, wood pigeons cooed in their cages hung high on bamboo poles behind the servants' quarters, a dog barked, chickens squawked and scratched in the yard and from the well came the splash of water. The wind blowing down from the mountains was cool and carried a faint smell of wood smoke from the *desas*. My mother poured us vanilla syrup in coloured glasses: red for me, green for Oeroeg. Ice tinkled against the rim. Even today the faintest whiff of vanilla is enough to bring it all flooding back to me: Oeroeg and me perched on the pebble-strewn steps of the back veranda sipping our drinks with great concentration, the ferns and flowers waving in the wind, and all around us the morning sounds from the sunny yard.

Two years after I was born my mother had a miscarriage, after which no further pregnancies ensued. Perhaps that was why Oeroeg was so exclusively my playmate, although Sidris went on to have child after child. The shared hours on the back veranda came to an end. Sometimes my mother sat there alone, writing letters or sewing, but more often I would find her in the filtered light of her bedroom, lying back in a cane chair with a moist handkerchief on her forehead. I sought and found entertainment with Oeroeg, either in the yard and around the house, or roaming beyond the fence, in the kampong and the adjacent tea gardens. We often spent the whole day with Sidris and Oeroeg's brothers and sisters at the *mandoer*'s quarters. Theirs was the only house in the kampong made of stone. The yard at the back was bounded by the river, which at this point was narrow and strewn with jutting stones. We children jumped from stone to stone, or waded in the shallows, where the water was crystal clear and as still as in a basin, and where we hunted for red and greeny-yellow crabs, dragonflies and other creatures. The shade of the dense growth fringing the banks teemed with insects. The younger children squatted naked in the pale brown mud, keeping very still while Oeroeg and I poked our sticks into the shadowy nooks behind the overhanging green.

We were about six years old at the time. I was the tallest, but Oeroeg, being thin and muscular, looked the older. In the line running from his shoulder-blades down to his narrow, straight hips you could already see the supple, confident strength of the half-grown boys and young men in the fields and at the factory. He could crouch down with his strong toes flexed to keep his balance on rocks and branches, more secure in his stance than I ever was, and quicker to react when instability threatened. Not that I was aware of such things in those days – I was too absorbed in our play. But I do recall disliking my freckles, and hating it when my arms turned all red and blistery in the scorching sun, and how envious I was of Oeroeg's dark skin, evenly coloured all over except for some faint pink blemishes resulting from an earlier skin disease. Oeroeg's face was flat and broad like his mother's, but without the gentle cheerfulness that made hers so appealing. I cannot remember his eyes ever losing that tense, searching gaze, as though forever listening out for a sound, a signal, that no one but he could hear. Oeroeg's eyes were so dark that even the surrounding whites seemed shadowy. In laughter or anger he narrowed his eyes, so that their sparkle was hidden by the ruff of short, stiff lashes. Like most natives Oeroeg never opened his mouth wide to laugh. In a burst of uncontrollable mirth he would rock silently to and fro, screwing his face up into a grimace.

The things we delighted in were not always the same. When I sprang over the stones in the river, whooping with excitement over an exceptional catch – a crab, pale pink and marbled like a shell, or a transparent salamander –

Oeroeg merely stared with his tense, dark look, flaring his nostrils slightly. He had a way with animals, catching them and carrying them around without ever getting hurt. I preferred to keep them in boxes and tins covered by a sheet of glass, and my mother, despite her abhorrence of 'beasties', had given me permission to store my collection in one of the outbuildings. But Oeroeg took little pleasure in the regular care and maintenance of such a menagerie. His attention flagged where mine began. He liked to tease a crab with a straw until the creature braced itself for attack. Most of all he liked to set up fights between animals of differing species, bringing toads to pit their strength against river and land crabs, goading tarantulas to fight with salamanders, wasps with dragonflies. It would be going too far to speak of cruelty here. Oeroeg was not cruel, it was simply that he did not know the feeling Europeans often have of wanting to spare an animal and treat it with respect, out of a half-conscious sense of affinity. Whenever I cried out, overcome partly by excitement and partly by guilt and horror at these gladiatorial sports, Oeroeg would throw me a sideways look of surprise, saying, as though to soothe me: 'What does it matter? They're only animals.' Our favourite pastime was pretending to be hunters and explorers, prowling around the fruit trees in the yard at the back, or, if we felt more adventurous, around the stony riverbed.

When my father was away on business or my mother suffering yet another attack of migraine, I had my meals at Oeroeg's house. Sidris, aging rapidly and somewhat shapeless after all her pregnancies, would be squatting among the pots and pans at the back with some female relative, frying pancakes stuffed with rice and meat in hot oil. Around them sat the children, quietly eating whatever Sidris slid towards them on a banana leaf. Skinny chickens pecked at the spilt grains of rice; the black dog, ever mangy, slunk about at a distance, waiting for us to finish and leave. I felt at home at her house, where the air was scented with the coconut oil she smoothed into her hair-knot. In the front porch stood some old, deep-seated rocking chairs – a gift from my mother. Paper fans and coloured pictures cut out of magazines were pinned to the whitewashed walls of woven bamboo. What I liked best was the Japanese bead curtain screening the entrance to the two small bedrooms. It showed Mount Fuji in an improbable shade of turquoise, with bright pink blossoms on sea-green trees in the foreground. When you passed through the screen, the beaded strings fell together behind you with a mysterious swishing sound. Oeroeg's grandfather spent his days ensconced in one of the rocking chairs, wearing striped cotton pyjamas and a sarong loosely draped over his shoulders. He was in his dotage, and did little but nod his head and laugh from time to time, baring the stumps of his teeth, which were stained dark red with betel juice. In front of the house was a yard separated from the rest of the kampong by a low whitened wall. Oeroeg and I copied my mother's gardener in marking out flowerbeds, though not with rows of whitened stones or decorative flowerpots, but with bottles which we buried neck down in the reddish soil so that only the concave bottoms showed. No grass grew in Sidris's garden, nor trees, but our flowerbeds were no less appealing for that.

Oeroeg came to my house too, now and then, but neither of us much enjoyed those visits. Any kind of rough game was out of the question because of my mother, and we were far too restless for construction kits or picture books. When the rains came, turning the garden into a swamp and the paths into mountain torrents, we would sit on the steps of the back veranda with our toes stretched out into the spray of droplets bouncing up from the gutter. Streams gushed from the rainspouts into the ditches and on towards the well in a monotonous minor key while the frogs croaked all day long, and apart from this no other sound could be heard beneath the low, slate-grey clouds hiding the mountain-tops.

In the rainy season my father spent more time at home. He sat in the inner gallery that served as his study, sometimes with my mother, but more often alone. Oeroeg and I were served food at a separate table and at a different hour than my parents. I seldom ate with my father and mother in the evenings, and never felt at ease on those occasions. Under the low-hanging lamp the dinner table resembled an island of desolation in the vast gloom of the back veranda. Now and then my parents exchanged a few words in muted tones, usually concerning domestic affairs, the factory, or the employees. The *djongos* padded back and forth between the pantry and the table, his head-cloth crisply folded like a crown. Each time he leaned over to serve me I caught a whiff of sweet tobacco blended with laundry starch, the smell forever trapped in his sarong and mess jacket. Sometimes my father quizzed me: whether I had been a good boy, what I had been up to during the day. I was always wary about my answers, for as likely as not they would spark off an argument between my parents. My father listened with a frown of displeasure to my halting account of our games and adventures.

'The boy shouldn't be in the kampong,' was his stock reply when I ran out of things to say. 'It does him no good at all. He can't utter a decent sentence in Dutch. Haven't you noticed? He's turning into a downright *katjang*. Why don't you keep him at home?'

'He should go to school,' my mother said one day, in response to such a tirade. 'He has turned six. How can I possibly keep him indoors? He needs to be kept busy; he needs to play. There aren't any other children here. He's always on his own.'

'Oeroeg!' I burst out, indignant at her failure to mention my best friend.

My mother shrugged.

'No school will accept him speaking the way he does,' my father said. 'Every other word is Soendanese. He'll have to learn some proper Dutch first.'

The subject was not pursued any further in my presence, but after a few days we received a visit from a young employee at the factory who, as I learned afterwards, had originally studied to be a teacher. It was explained to me that I would be prepared for entrance to primary school in Soekaboemi. I spluttered in protest. I knew Oeroeg was outside waiting for me – he had been sent away by my mother upon the arrival of my new tutor – because I had spotted his bright red shirt among the bushes by the servants' quarters. We had made a plan to dig up ant-lions. While my mother conversed with the young man I tried to slip away over the back veranda, without success. I was told to sit down and pay attention. I was to be asked a number of questions, which I had to answer in Dutch, not Soendanese. Oeroeg crept up to the steps of the back veranda and stood there motionless, staring in silent wonder until the 'lesson' came to an end.

That evening my mother came to my room at bedtime, which was a rare occurrence. I felt shy, and while I undressed and washed with the *baboe*'s help my mother informed me that the hours with Mr Bollinger would continue until the start of the new term in August. I said I did not want to go to school, believing it would mean having to sit still and answer questions. My mother listed the advantages of being a schoolboy, but the prospect of learning to read, write and do sums held little appeal for me.

'Will Oeroeg be going to school too?' I asked, when she had finished.

My mother sighed. She was sitting on a low cane chair

by the bed, wearing a flower-patterned kimono and wreathed as always in the scent of eau de cologne.

'What do you think?' she replied impatiently, dabbing her temples with a damp handkerchief. 'Don't be silly. Oeroeg is a native boy, you know that.'

'Doesn't *he* have to go to school then?' I persisted.

My mother stood up and gave me a fleeting kiss on the cheek.

'Perhaps,' she said vaguely. 'It would be a different school, of course. It's time you went to sleep now.'

I clambered up into bed and crouched on the mattress while the *baboe* tucked the mosquito net in on all sides.

'I'll ask Sidris . . .' I began, peering at my mother through the netting.

She paused by the door.

'I don't want you playing in the kampong any more,' she said in the peevish, nervous tone that signalled the onset of one of her migraines. 'Your father doesn't approve. You can ask Oeroeg to come and play here if you like. Sleep tight.'

And so it happened. I still managed to escape now and then, to the river and to Sidris's welcoming home, especially during my father's absences, but mostly Oeroeg came over to my house. We plundered the fruit trees in the garden, went hunting for all manner of game in the bushes of the neglected back yard, or, on rainy days, sat on our heels between the columns of the veranda doing things I cannot recall. When Mr Bollinger arrived for my lesson, Oeroeg settled himself on the ground not far away, never taking his eyes off us. He had reacted quite calmly to the news that I was to be sent to school, wanting only to know whether I would be going by train, and when I said yes began to imitate the noise of a locomotive, huffing and puffing with fanatical concentration. After that we never mentioned school or Mr Bollinger again. We both thought it perfectly normal for Oeroeg to be present during my instruction. My mother, who would wander in from time to time when Mr Bollinger was there, tried several times to send Oeroeg away. He pretended to do as he was told, but was back again in no time, lurking by the potted plants on the steps of the veranda.

My father seemed pleased with my progress in expanding my vocabulary. However, it was some time before I lost the thick accent of someone more at home in Soendanese than in Dutch. The months went by as preparations were made for my school attendance. An elderly native seamstress sat behind the treadle sewing machine in the inner gallery, where, under my mother's guidance, she fashioned the trousers and shirts that would replace my cotton playsuits. A Chinese shoemaker came to measure my feet for sandals. Finally my father returned from one of his trips with a satchel and other school necessities. I showed myself to Oeroeg, all kitted out. He looked me up and down, inspected the contents of my pencil-box and asked once more if I would be taking the train every day.

One evening my mother went about the house in formal dress and with her hair done up, which was not like her. The oil lamps in the inner gallery were lit and our *djongos* busied himself setting the table with a great variety of platters and refreshments. I heard that we were having guests: some ladies and gentlemen from Batavia, who were staying at a neighbouring estate. Mr Bollinger would be coming too.

'No, you won't be having a lesson,' my mother said, smiling as she paused in front of a mirror to assess her appearance. 'If you behave yourself, you can have dinner with the grown-ups.'

The *baboe* dressed me in one of my school outfits. Profoundly impressed by this unusual state of affairs, I waited in front of the house for the guests to arrive. It was just after sundown, and the trees bordering the garden stood sharply outlined against the red cloud-banks in the west. The mountaintops were still bathed in light. A soporific whirr of insects sounded from the darkness under bushes and trees. From the kampong came the beat of a hollow tree-trunk drum, signalling nightfall. As I stared at the fading glow on the horizon an unprecedented mood of unease stole over me – because school loomed, because from now on everything would be different. Whether I was at all aware of this at the time is doubtful, so my understanding of the cause of my melancholy and apprehension may well derive from hindsight.

Down on the main road a car turned in through the gate, and after a few minutes pulled up at the front veranda. My mother appeared and welcomed the guests. My father was with them. All I remember of the actual dinner is that my parents talked and laughed as never before, and that I was so astonished by this that I almost forgot the food. After the meal, when the company repaired to the inner gallery (I was sitting unnoticed on the floor next to the gramophone cabinet), someone suggested going for a drive to Telaga Hideung, further up the mountain. Hearing that name made my heart beat faster. The 'Black Lake' figured prominently in the fantasies Oeroeg and I wove together, largely thanks to its scary reputation among the locals. Telaga Hideung, in the middle of the jungle, was a gathering place of evil spirits and dead souls. Nènèh Kombèl lived there: a vampire in the guise of an old woman, who preyed on dead children.

A cousin of Oeroeg's named Satih, who lived with Sidris, was a teller of spine-chilling stories, all connected in one way or another with the Black Lake. We pictured it as an inky expanse of water where monsters and ghosts held sway. We would go there when we grew up and do battle with them. Sometimes, sitting on our haunches for a rest from playing, or sheltering from a shower, we would spin out this future expedition in gruesome detail, shivering with pleasurable fright. I had been to Telaga Hideung once before, as a very young child, but my only recollection of that excursion was seeing my father in a bathing costume. The lake served as a swimming pool for the employees of the estate, but it was too far away to be used very often. Now Mr Bollinger, pointing to the bright orange disc of the full moon behind the leafy treetops, suggested taking a swim there. The plan met with wide approval, and everybody rose to their feet. I sidled up to my mother and tugged at her skirt. Her face was flushed and her eyes shone. She had something strange about her that evening, and beautiful, with her long pendant ear-rings and upswept hair.

'What, not in bed yet?' she said, smiling distractedly. 'Would you like to come with us?'

Just then my father emerged from the bedroom with an armful of bathing togs. He frowned and raised objections, but the rest of the company, laughing and joking – there were a great many empty glasses on the table – persuaded him to let me come along. I trembled with anticipation. It was a shame Oeroeg would be missing this, but on the other hand I felt a surge of pride that I should be the first to go there, even if it was under supervision. The grown-ups displayed remarkably high spirits, as though it were a pleasure trip we were embarking on, and I secretly admired them for it. The houseboy was dispatched to the *mandoer*'s house to fetch Deppoh, Oeroeg's father. I had no idea why, but did not dare enquire, nor did I dare ask if Oeroeg could come with us, in case they decided to leave me behind at the last minute.

Finally we all piled into the car. I stood leaning against Mr Bollinger's knees. Oeroeg's father and Danoeh the gardener posted themselves on the running-boards on either side, and off we went. I stared at Deppoh, whom I did not know very well. I was much in awe of him, almost as much as of my father. He was the most handsome native I have ever seen, slender and tall, with beautifully chiselled features. He stood upright on the running-board, holding on with only one hand. The moon shone on his white, starched jacket. I felt he was looking down disapprovingly at the boisterous passengers. One of our guests launched into a long story, the point of which was lost on me, though it elicited gales of laughter. My mother lounged back in the corner between Mr Bollinger and the side of the car, with her head resting against the folds of the open hood. Tears of laughter glistened on her cheeks. I felt uncomfortable wedged against my tutor's knees, and tried to sit on the edge of the back seat, between him and my mother. Pushing my mother's skirt aside I saw that she and Mr Bollinger were holding hands.

The night sky was metallic blue, spangled with stars. The moon stood higher now, and had lost the russet glow it had had earlier. The wind sifted through the grass and the thickets of bamboo on either side of the road, which wound its way up the mountainside in wide curves. Now and then we had a full view of the plain below, where the flooded *sawahs* glittered between black clumps of trees, and a few tiny lights flickered in a remote *desa*. Seen from above, the tea gardens with their long rows of uniform shrubs resembled flocks of orderly sheep, unmoving in the moonlight, lightly shaded at the edges by the lacy albizia trees.

As we drove on we heard the clatter of falling water. Between the mossy rocks on the steep slope trickled sparkling rivulets, which converged into a brook by the wayside. The air at this altitude was almost cold, smelling of moist earth and decaying leaves. Around a bend in the road began the jungle, and we entered the gloom amid much laughter and raillery. I squatted down on the floor of the car, fearful of the darkness throbbing with the sounds of the night. Only the proximity of Deppoh, standing stock-still on the running-board, gave me a sense of security. It seemed to me that the others, with all their noise and jollity, had no notion of the perils of this realm of demons. But Deppoh knew. Looking up at his distinct profile, which I glimpsed each time a ray of moonlight pierced the canopy, I was sure of it.

The car stopped, and everyone got out. I kept close to Deppoh, who led the way through the tall undergrowth with a pocket torch. We followed a narrow, stony path leading steeply upwards. The air was filled with rustling sounds, as though a gang of invisible beings was keeping pace with us as we climbed the mountain. Something streaked away through the branches overhead.

'A flying squirrel,' Deppoh said.

Holding on tight to the hem of his sarong, I whispered, still quaking with fright, 'Not Nèneh Kombèl?'

'Of course not!' Deppoh replied, his voice a little gruff, but no less resolute for that. 'The *sinjo besar* should have been in bed long ago.'

He stopped and turned round, lighting the path with his torch for the others to catch up. They advanced in single file. My mother and Mr Bollinger were the last to arrive, whereupon we all set off again. It was as though we were entering a tunnel of complete darkness, pierced only by the thin beam of Deppoh's torch. I kept close to him, saying nothing and trying hard not to be scared of the noises in the undergrowth.

'Won't Oeroeg be going to school?' I ventured at last. The thought of Oeroeg seemed to bring a shred of reality into this pitch-black nocturnal world.

'Maybe,' replied Deppoh.

In the distance we saw a white gleam. When we drew near I saw it came from moonbeams slanting through the trees.

'Look, there's Telaga Hideung,' Deppoh said quietly.

My heart pounded in my throat, but there was no going back. My father and two other men began to run, wagering which of them would be the first to reach the lake. I felt embarrassed, and spied anxiously left and right for stalking ghosts. From afar came the echoing laughter of the runners. My mother, Mr Bollinger and another lady overtook us now. With Deppoh and Danoeh on either side of me, I walked in the moonlight to the water's edge. I felt a strong sense of disappointment. What I saw was not the vast expanse of black water of my imagination, but a pool, hardly more than a large pond, completely encircled by steep, thickly wooded slopes. The treetops, some like filigree, some fluffy like wool, shone pale blue in the moonlight. The lake made me think of the shiny base of a vase shaped like a truncated cone. Water plants floated on the surface, especially along the edges. Leafy branches and lianas trailed in the water. The thousand-voiced drone of insects and the cries of nocturnal jungle creatures all seemed to be part of the same overwhelming silence. Over the mountain peaks shone stars of an icy brilliance. I stared at the far side of the Black Lake, where the foliage touched the surface. I could easily imagine evil spirits lurking there, poised for ambush. When Deppoh and Danoeh ventured some way into the darkness, I reluctantly stayed behind with my mother and the others.

It now dawned on me why Oeroeg's father and the gardener had come along. I heard a soft splash in the lake, and a raft came gliding towards us, punted forth by the two men. At a point where the bank was least marshy we stepped on board. The raft consisted of thin planks lashed to hollow bamboo poles, on top of which was fixed a small two-level hut, likewise of bamboo. While the ladies settled themselves on an old cane bench and the men went into the hut to change into their swimming costumes we drifted slowly towards the middle of the lake. Danoeh moved back and forth as he poled the raft, with Deppoh giving low-voiced directions and taking soundings in search of a suitable place for swimming. My father and his guests laughed rowdily inside the bamboo hut. I stood beside the ladies on the bench, staring intently at the shore of the lake, where every sound, every tremor of the leaves in the moonlight seemed to have some supernatural cause. Swimming in the lake seemed to me to be a dangerous and pointless exercise – had Satih not said that it was thousands of metres deep, and home to a gigantic serpent? Circles kept forming on the surface for no apparent reason, with the moonlight gleaming on the expanding ripples. Was there something moving in the depths? I cried out in terror when a pale shape surfaced alongside the raft, and was only partially reassured by the hilarity it caused among the rest of the company. It was Mr Bollinger, who had soundlessly slipped into the water to give us all a fright.

The men's bodies glimmered white in the moonlight. They dived in one after another and came up gasping and spluttering. The mountain vase was suddenly filled with the sound of echoing voices and splashing water. I could not understand how they could be so jolly, so carefree. Danoeh kept the raft floating in the same place while Deppoh sat on his heels in the shadow of the bamboo hut – I could just see the tip of his cigarette glowing in the dark. His relaxed air made me feel a little less anxious, and I went to sit beside him.

'Is it true that Nènèh Kombèl eats children?' I whispered.

'Ach,' said Deppoh with a hint of irritation in his voice. He did not answer my question, but leaned forward to call out a warning to the bathers. 'Water plants,' he said to me, by way of explanation. 'It's only safe to swim near the raft. The water plants catch hold of a man and won't let go, so that he drowns. I know all about Telaga Hideung.'

I stared at the water in fascination, and wished that my father would come out, onto the safety of the raft. My wish was soon granted, as the deepening chill of the night drove the bathers out of the water. They stood around on deck, snorting and stamping their feet as they rubbed themselves dry with towels. Then, in a burst of elation, they began to leapfrog around the ladies on the bench. The planks underfoot creaked; the entire raft rocked and shook.

'Take care! The bamboo is old!' Deppoh shouted in warning, but nobody took any notice.

Someone chanted 'What shall we do with the drunken sailor?' and they all rounded on Mr Bollinger, jokingly threatening to heave him overboard. My tutor fled into the hut and climbed onto the flat roof, with my father and two other men in hot pursuit, cheered on by the ladies. I was thrilled by the chase, and went over to the far side of the raft to see how Mr Bollinger was faring. That is all I remember. There was a great noise of splitting bamboo, people shouting and screaming, and I toppled over, headlong into ice-cold darkness.

When I came to, I was lying in bed at home. Through the white mist of the mosquito net I could see a small light burning. My father was standing at the foot of my bed, looking at me. I had no idea what had taken place. My first thought was that I must have been dreaming about the lake and the moonlight, but my hair was damp and I seemed to have a taste of mud in my mouth. I stirred and cried out. My father drew the netting aside, and the *baboe* appeared beside him, holding out a glass of steaming liquid. I drank it down, leaning against my father. I fell asleep again at once.

It was not until several days later that I learned what had happened. The raft, already over-laden, had not been up to the strain of a succession of men wrestling their way up the bamboo elevation. The old, mould-infested planking had given way, and the top-heavy part of the raft had broken off, capsized and vanished under water. All the men had surfaced again quite quickly, shocked and injured by bamboo splinters and broken planks. Only I was still missing. Deppoh had dived into the water to search for me among the floating wreckage. Not long afterwards my father had found me, half-choked, among the debris of woven bamboo, after which we had all returned to the shore on the remainder of the raft.

'What about Deppoh?' I asked, my heart racing with a presentiment of disaster.

'Deppoh got caught in the water plants,' my father

replied slowly and very softly, as though preferring me not to hear. 'Deppoh died.'

A worse calamity could not have befallen me. Worst of all was the realization that Deppoh had lost his life trying to save mine. I could not stop thinking about the water plants he had told me about on the lake that night. At all hours of the day and night I was tormented by ghastly visions of his body writhing amid tough, viscous stems. Time and again I woke up screaming. I was feverishly conscious of figures at my bedside: my mother, Mr Bollinger with a bandage round his head, my father.

At last Oeroeg too came to visit, but we barely spoke. Oeroeg was ever quiet and shy in the presence of adults, and now he was further intimidated by my illness and the hushed atmosphere of my darkened bedroom. I was racked with guilt at having been the cause of his father's death. We stared at each other wordlessly.

'Oeroeg has come to say goodbye to you,' my mother said. 'He's moving away.' She went on to explain that the stone house by the river was needed for the new *mandoer*, and that Sidris and the children would be going to live with a relative in one of the *desas* further up the mountain.

I never discovered what tipped the balance in the end:

my own despair at the prospect of being parted from Oeroeg, my parents' sense of responsibility towards Deppoh's son, or possibly the maternal solicitude and ambition shown by the gentle Sidris. One day, for the first time since I was a toddler, she came to the house again, impeccably dressed with a fragrant bloom in her hair-knot and a dusting of talcum powder on her brow. She was with my mother for a long time. I could hear their voices in the bedroom next to mine, but not what they were saying. Whatever it was they discussed, it had far-reaching consequences. The outcome was that Oeroeg would be staying on at the estate, living with our house-boy, who was a second cousin of Deppoh's, and that he would attend the Dutch Native School in Soekaboemi.

Looking back on our time at primary school, the days of all those years seem to conflate into a single image, no doubt because the various impressions succeeded one another so regularly and unchangingly. Early each morning the car took us to the little station, half an hour's drive from the estate. Grass and foliage glistened in the heavy dew, the sun had barely risen and a blue morning haze hung over the countryside. People were taking fruit and other wares to the station. Weighed down by their heavily laden *pikolans* they trotted slowly and rhythmically along the road. A farmer drove his water buffaloes to the *sawah*, with the assistance of small boys uttering shrill cries to keep the beasts in order. Oeroeg knew some of them, and shouted greetings as he leaned out of the car window. From the opposite direction came parties of tea pickers and plantation workers. The women looked round at us and smiled from beneath the folds of the *slendang*s they wore wrapped round their heads. Children, dogs and chickens came running from the cluster of dwellings in the shade of the tall trees.

The station was always very busy. There were piles of baskets and crowds of people waiting for the first train, and there was a stall with early refreshments on sale. Oeroeg and I often treated ourselves to a portion of *roedjak*, unripe fruit served with a hot sauce, which we slurped up hastily from a folded leaf. Then the train came in: the small mountain locomotive with its string of carriages, windowless but furnished with long wooden benches. Although Oeroeg and I had permission to travel second class we preferred the crowded carriages, where we were often offered a piece of fruit or a handful of peanuts and where there was always something interesting going on. Of that railway line through the Preanger highlands I know every stone, every telegraph pole, every bridge. With my eyes closed I would be able to draw the landscape on either side: the slopes terraced with *sawahs*, the thickly wooded, cone-shaped hills rising into blue mountain ranges beyond, the harvest shelters in the fields, the *desa* cottages amid thickets of bamboo, the little stations we passed, whitewashed and bustling with market folk. By the time we arrived in Soekaboemi the sun was already brutal, dividing the world into glaring light and cool shade. We walked a little way through the city – to us Soekaboemi was a city – and then our ways parted: Oeroeg went to his school, I to mine.

There was little difference in what we were taught – only that Oeroeg had Dutch as an extra subject. The hours we spent in our respective classrooms must have been much the same: the constant drone of children reciting a lesson in chorus, the accompanying sound of shuffling feet, the scratch of slate-pencils and pens, while outside the trees rustled in the breeze and the hot air quivered above the asphalt of the high street. At one o'clock we met up again at our fixed meeting place. As I came running I could see Oeroeg waiting for me in the shade of a tree, barefoot, but in my view smartly dressed in velvet trousers and boy-scout belt. On his head he wore the Muslim black cap. We often spent a few cents on goodies to eat on the train: brightly coloured ice lollipops frozen fast around sticks so that you could suck them, or we indulged our fancy for an extremely sticky delicacy of coconut-flavoured pudding. At this time of the day it was very hot, even at the higher altitude of Kebon Djati, and the first thing we did when we got home was cool ourselves off, me in the bathroom and Oeroeg at the well behind the outbuildings.

After school we still played the same old games in the garden and by the river, but we gradually began to take an interest in other things. We collected stamps, cigar bands and pictures of cars and aeroplanes. Oeroeg was especially fascinated by the latter. His imitation of the screech of a plane coming in to land was highly realistic. He ran around in circles with his arms stretched wide, he jumped, crouched and crawled, and finally, shrieking and sputtering at full volume, fell flat on the ground. My own efforts were no match for his. There was a shyness, or embarrassment, or an inability to lose myself so fully in make-believe that prevented me from expressing myself in cries and gestures the way Oeroeg did. It was at this stage that I discovered the joys of reading, a pastime that Oeroeg was less taken by, although he liked books with illustrations. He excelled at drawing, displaying a keen preference for the symmetrical figures of the school books: circles and triangles ingeniously drawn through and about each other, which he would fill with bright colours.

As I took Oeroeg's presence for granted I was as yet unaware of his unconventional status within our household: somewhere between that of a member of the family and a domestic. He ate and slept in the servants' quarters, but spent the greater part of the day with me. My mother calmly let this take its course. It was not until much later that I realised that the friendship between Oeroeg and me was a relief to her. She had become more outgoing lately, and had bought herself a horse. She often went riding on the estate with Mr Bollinger. My father was very busy, and frequently away from home for days at a stretch. On Sundays Oeroeg went to visit his mother, and I usually accompanied him. Sidris and the younger children now occupied a tiny *desa* dwelling, which seemed surprisingly run-down and dirty in comparison with their old house by the river. Oeroeg's grandfather had died in the meantime, and the rocking chairs had disappeared with him; only the Japanese beaded screen recalled past glories The children's clothes were dirty and threadbare. They all crowded around us whenever we came, bursting with admiration and curiosity but too shy to ply Oeroeg with questions. But he needed no encouragement. Surrounded by relatives and inquisitive neighbours, he would launch into detailed accounts of his life on the estate, of the train, of Soekaboemi, of the lessons at school. Sidris, looking older and more careworn now, listened to her son with pride, uttering little exclamations from time to time, or clicking her tongue in that way of hers that could express a whole range of emotions. While Oeroeg held forth, his cousin Satih, who had moved up the mountain with Sidris and the children, would take the little ones in turn and plant them between her knees to pick the lice from their hair. Satih was a pretty girl of about sixteen, almost too plump in her faded sarong.

Never did I feel myself an outsider among these people, quite the opposite in fact. In that shabby little abode with its muddy yard I felt more at home than in the dark, echoing rooms of my house. After each visit, as Oeroeg and I went back down the stony path to the plantation, I felt as though I had just said goodbye to my own family. It never occurred to me to question where Oeroeg and I stood with regard to each other. To my mind we were completely equal. I might have had a vague notion of difference in race and station where the houseboy, the *baboe* and Danoeh were concerned, but Oeroeg's existence and mine were so intertwined that I never felt that way about him. So I was all the more surprised to find, as time went on, that the familiarity between Oeroeg and me and my parents was frowned on and ridiculed by our servants. Initially this was expressed in trivial ways, such as addressing him teasingly as 'Mr Oeroeg', sniggering among themselves, a sarcastic word or gesture, but gradually their disapproval took the form of more or less open resistance.

I now knew too that my father was paying for Oeroeg's schooling, which I thought obvious, considering the way Deppoh had died. How Oeroeg felt about all this remained unclear. He was always the same, and went in and out of our house as well as the outbuildings without the least demurral. I cannot imagine how lost I would have been if Oeroeg had not been there.

Without him I would no doubt have been far more distressed by the separation of my parents. I had been left almost entirely in the care of the *baboe* from an early age, and had spent so much time with Sidris and her family – and with Oeroeg – that my mother was little more than a stranger to me. After the Telaga Hideung debacle her initial loneliness and frequent headaches passed into a period of restlessness and almost feverish activity. She went riding; she took long walks; she visited the shops in Soekaboemi. For days on end the old seamstress set the needle of the sewing machine dancing up and down on new dress-materials while my mother drifted nervously from room to room, now and then dropping into a chair to tear up letters or play a game of patience. Sometimes there would be guests staying at the house, but it was usually Mr Bollinger keeping my mother company: at teatime, in the evenings, or during strolls around the tea gardens. Gradually I became aware of a growing coolness between my parents, whose relationship had not been particularly affectionate at the best of times. Lying in bed at night I heard doors slam and voices raised in anger. One day I sought out my mother in the garden – she had said she was going to feed the pigeons – and I came upon her sobbing. Shortly after that Mr Bollinger left for Europe. It was years later that I began to suspect a con-nection between the two events, both of which I dismissed at the time as simply beyond comprehension.

When my father finally announced that my mother would be going away for an indefinite period, I registered the news, bewildering though it was, as just another of those facts of life that a child apparently had no choice but to accept. Oeroeg, however, seemed secretly amused when I told him, and made a remark I did not understand. Later it became clear to me that the servants had their eyes about them at all times, and that through them Oeroeg had been well aware of what went on in our house. He never mentioned it to me, then or later, when we were of an age to discuss such things. All I ever noticed back then was the shadow of mockery and disdain crossing his face whenever my mother's name was mentioned.

Her departure was preceded by days of hectic agitation. The inner gallery was filled with trunks and packing cases, into which a large part of our household goods and linens disappeared. My father did not show his face. Then one morning the car drove up, followed by a lorry from the factory, into which the luggage was loaded. The tears and embraces of my mother, who was not normally given to such displays of emotion, threw me so completely off balance that I howled with anguish when the car drove away. I had been given the day off from school for the occasion, but Oeroeg had gone to Soekaboemi as usual. I wandered aimlessly about the house, which, stripped of so many pictures, vases and doilies, seemed even chillier than before. In the inner gallery I saw that the chairs were still pushed to one side to make room for all the packing cases. Straw and wood shavings littered the floor. As I stood surveying the desolation, my father returned from the factory, where he had taken refuge for the duration. He sank down on one of the chairs with a sigh and mopped the perspiration from his face and neck. For the first time in my life I saw in him something other than the authority, the stern judge, the supreme ruler of my childish existence. I noticed that the hair on his crown was thinning, and that he looked weary and apprehensive.

'Ah,' my father said evenly, 'there you are. Some change, eh? We must tell the boy to sweep up this mess.' He patted me absent-mindedly on the shoulder. 'Off you go now and play,' he continued, and, when I hung back, added: 'I was going to take you with me into the gardens this afternoon, but I'm afraid someone's coming to see me at the factory.'

'Oh, when Oeroeg gets back we're going fishing,' I said quickly, to reassure him.

My father frowned a moment, and sighed again.

'Fine, fine,' he said, standing up to go to the bedroom. 'Run along and play with Oeroeg then.'

And so began a new stage in our lives. I was then in the fourth year of primary school.

One of the major events to take place in those years, as far as we were concerned, was the arrival of Gerard Stokman, the employee who was to replace Mr Bollinger. He was an exceptionally tall and thin young man, with a face seemingly carved from pale brown, shiny wood. He turned up at the estate in a khaki suit with short trousers. His legs were bony and hairy, and he was wearing gym shoes. His luggage consisted for the most part of hunting equipment: guns, small-bore rifles, knives, poles with metal mounts, fishing nets and rods, stained and scruffy game-bags, a tent and an assortment of camping gear packed in canvas bags, in addition to several crates containing stuffed animals and cured animal skins. Needless to say, Oeroeg and I watched in breathless wonder as the lorry was being unloaded.

Gerard Stokman was assigned a small pavilion not far from our house. Once everything had been carried into his new home, he dismissed the coolies and began to unpack. He seemed to think it perfectly natural that Oeroeg and I should be present, and allowed us to help him store and arrange his belongings. He asked our advice about where to hang his collection of Dayak weaponry, which, with their sharp teeth and barbed hooks, Oeroeg found particularly compelling. Wielding one of these assegais he would stalk imaginary enemies to the furthest corners of the pavilion, by turns playing the hunter and the hunted. I squatted down among the glass-eyed stuffed animals, whose gaping maws were varnished red inside. There was a monkey, a small panther, a flying squirrel, an alligator, birds, lizards and a glass box full of preserved snakes. There were jam jars sealed with parchment and containing yellow liquid in which floated unidentifiable parts of animals, pieces of skin and suchlike. The keeper of all these treasures stepped up onto a chair to nail the skin of an anteater to the wall. He answered our questions tirelessly, and told us about himself. He was the son of an army officer in Bandoeng, and had lost his heart to Java, to hunting and to the outdoor life. He was at loggerheads with his parents, since they objected to his choice of career, but he seemed to take all this quite philosophically.

'It will turn out for the best, or not, as the case may be,' he said. 'We'll just have to wait and see. I need to have space around me. I'm not one for the life of offices and barracks, and I have no desire to go to Holland either. I've been there a few times, with my father on furlough, and that was quite enough for me. This is a wonderful place. Did you know it's teeming with wild boar out there? Next Saturday I mean to go up the mountain, given half a chance.'

Chances there were many. Not a weekend went by without our seeing Gerard (as we took to calling him almost from the start) strike up the path through the tea gardens towards the mountain forest with his rifle and knife, followed by a coolie carrying a tent and provisions. These expeditions held Oeroeg and me spellbound. We passed countless evenings at the pavilion, where Gerard would smoke his pipe and talk to us while he cleaned and polished his gun or occupied himself with his hunting trophies. He told us he had buried a boar's head in the garden – a cleaning job for the ants. Oeroeg and I were greatly intrigued by how long this process would take, and after a few weeks suggested digging the head up to see how far things had progressed. Gerard advised strongly that we wait another month and, sure enough, at the end of this interval the skull emerged almost stripped bare (though decidedly smelly) from its place of interment. The prize was scrubbed clean and given a coat of colourless varnish, after which Gerard presented it to Oeroeg and me as a gift. It was our most treasured possession, which we took turns to keep on our bedside tables, and which we brought to school from time to time to impress our classmates.

But this was nothing compared to the joy we felt when Gerard offered to take us with him on one of his weekly expeditions. With knives tucked into our belts and blanket-rolls strapped to our backs we followed our leader up the steep, stony paths into the jungle, where the majestic tree crowns high overhead intermingled to form an uninterrupted green roof, impenetrable to the sun. We felt as if we were making our way through the murky light of an aquarium. There was a pungent odour of damp leaves, of layers of vegetation decaying slowly into black soil. There were ice-cold trickles of clear water in the undergrowth, tiny streams as wide as a man's hand, rivulets coursing through a bed strewn with grey stones polished smooth by the water. All around us was the splash of falling water, and the air felt saturated with droplets. Awed by the stillness under this vast dome of greenery, Oeroeg and I spoke only in whispers at first. There was much to be frightened of in the shadowy depths of thickly overgrown clefts in the mountainside and in tree trunks that had been twisted and carbonised by lightning, but the lanky figure of Gerard ahead of us inspired boundless confidence.

On the saddle between two mountain peaks he had discovered an old cabin, which he had promoted to hunting lodge. This residence owed its fantastical appearance to the repairs undertaken by Gerard. Lids of biscuit tins, pieces of wood in all sorts of shapes and colours, and coarsely woven aerial roots cut down in the forest had all been used to cover holes in the top and the sides; a wall on the point of collapse was propped up by a neat pile of stones. Inside the hut there were two built-in bunk beds, which Gerard called 'the rabbit hutches', a wonky table and a few tree stumps to serve as seats. A row of nails knocked into the sturdiest part of the wall provided the only storage facility. This was where we hung our mugs, clothing and weapons. From under one of the bunks Gerard pulled out a battered charcoal burner, which he proceeded to install on the patch of scorched earth in front of the cabin, beneath the overhang of the roof. Our cooking equipment consisted of one saucepan and an empty margarine tin. Ali, the coolie who always accompanied Gerard, went off to collect firewood while Oeroeg and I drew water from the brook behind the cabin, where, with a purpose-built waterfall and a length of hollowed-out bamboo, Gerard had fashioned a water conduit that proved invaluable for all manner of domestic activities.

The acrid, smoky smell of burning wood remains for me indissolubly linked with the remembrance of those mealtimes by the cabin: Gerard sitting on a slice of tree trunk stirring the contents of a tin of corned beef into the pan of rice; Ali squatting down, dangling his forearms over his wide-spread knees; Oeroeg and me panting with excitement and hunger; and before us, beyond the craggy incline of the mountain saddle, over the tops of the jungle trees further down, the rolling mountainscape in every shade of blue, grey and green, with inky streaks indicating clefts and ravines, and further down still the plain, over which the drifting clouds cast huge shadows all the way to the heat haze blurring the horizon.

In the afternoon Gerard inspected the look-outs he had built in the brushwood and the trees to spy on the wild animals. He showed us a platform made of bamboo between two branches of a tree.

'That's where we're going tonight to wait for the wild boar,' he said. 'They won't detect our scent so far off the ground.'

Towards evening it grew chilly. Gerard, who always thought of everything, rummaged in his bag and produced woollen jumpers for us, in which we all but disappeared. A thick mist crept up on all sides from the ravines, seemingly shutting us off from the plain below. We were not accustomed to this teeth-chattering cold, but Gerard kept us busy and sent us into the forest with Ali for new supplies of firewood. At nightfall we sat around the fire Gerard had lit in front of the cabin. We spoke Soendanese on account of Oeroeg and Ali – indeed, using the vernacular became a habit. On these occasions the otherwise taciturn coolie, normally so self-effacing as to blend into the background, proved himself to be a born storyteller.

'Just listen to him,' said Gerard, with the pride of an impresario. 'He knows dozens of stories.'

Ali was compliant. He moved a little closer to the fire and drew the striped blanket over his shoulders. His gestures were so solemn as to appear ceremonial. He spoke softly, without all the gradations of volume and intonation that are generally considered essential to good storytelling. But never had I heard a story recounted more compellingly. Ali's voice possessed the same quality as the nocturnal stillness all around us, the sound of falling water in the forest, the wind in the treetops. We had no trouble at all imagining ourselves in that shadowy domain of animal fables and myths of demigods and supernatural beings. Oeroeg was already familiar with some of the tales, and would interrupt from time to time to supply a name or another detail – prematurely, in the opinion of Ali, whose reaction to such forward behaviour was to stop in mid-sentence and spit in the fire. Only after an expectant silence on the part of his audience, during which I nudged Oeroeg to keep quiet, would he resume his narrative.

We went to bed early – not that we got much sleep on the planking of the bunks, each of which could accommodate four people. Wrapped up in our blankets we listened to the sounds of the night outside: the pelting clatter of the cascade behind the cabin and the soughing wind in the trees lulling us into a sort of half-slumber, which seemed to have lasted only a few seconds when Gerard announced it was time to get up. This was usually between three and four o'clock.

Oeroeg and I were ready in a flash, and too excited to feel in the least tired. In the light of Gerard's pocket torch our shadows danced wildly and ghost-like on the cabin walls. After an admonishment to tread softly and not to talk once we were in the thick of the trees we set off in single file, Gerard in front and Ali bringing up the rear. At first, the ominous gloom of the jungle made Oeroeg and me forget all the plans we had made in anticipation of our expedition. Gone was our determination to steal through the undergrowth brandishing our knives, fully prepared to attack panthers and wild boar, and it was not until we were safely ensconced on the platform in the tree that we felt intrepid once more. The jungle seemed alive with rustling sounds, but Ali, who was in charge of the torch, told us to have patience. He shone the torch into the blackness from time to time, and if we were lucky, we spotted a wild boar or two, or even a whole herd of them in a break between the trees. The air would reverberate with the sound of gunshots followed by a rush of snapping twigs and the scurrying sound of animals in flight.

In those days – and for a long time afterwards – Gerard was our leader, our mainstay, the infallible authority on every difficulty we encountered. He was regarded as eccentric by the other employees, for he neither drank nor played bridge and had no interest in weekly visits to the club in Soekaboemi. He was one of those people to whom complete solitude is congenial. He was always busy with something when we went round to his pavilion in the evening. He liked us, and treated us as housemates from whom he had no secrets. We spoke Dutch and Soendanese by turns, depending on circumstances. Oeroeg understood Dutch and could read it too, but was shy about expressing himself in the language. When we urged him to do so anyway, he would make an embarrassed grimace and mumble a refusal. However, not a word escaped him of the conversations Gerard and I held in Dutch.

I had less contact than ever with my father. He worked long hours at the factory and did not return until late in the afternoon. Most days I only saw him at the dinner table. He ate quickly, usually in silence. His thoughts were elsewhere: on his work, presumably, or on concerns I had no conception of. He had lost weight, and looked gaunt in the face. His hairline had receded further, and from his nostrils to the corners of his mouth and chin ran two sharp furrows, which made him look severe and yet somehow vulnerable. I was aware that he was known on the estate as someone demanding a strong sense of duty and as a stickler for discipline, to whom any error or negligence – whether committed by himself or a subordinate – was intolerable. The sporadic moods of almost boyish jollity, of laughing and quipping with employees or guests, belonged to the past. Indeed, there were no guests any more, and since the Bollinger affair my father seemed to have put a greater distance between himself and his employees. After the evening meal my father withdrew to the inner gallery, which, divested now of everything that served no specific purpose, was as lacking in character as a room in a hotel. He would sit there and smoke, or read one of the dog-eared detective stories or Wild West novels with garish covers left behind by the previous manager. Now and then he played a gramophone record – even then I felt, although only half-consciously, that there could be nothing sadder than listening to marching band music and waltzes from operettas in the chill of a house that is not a home.

When Oeroeg and I were not with Gerard at the pavilion, we sat at the table on the back veranda with our sums and grammars. My father would stop by sometimes and look over our shoulders, take up our exercise books and ask about our progress. He always scrutinised the school reports Oeroeg and I brought home before adding his signature, but as we never got bad marks he had no cause to comment. Oeroeg's handwriting was exceptionally good, in precise imitation of the examples given in school, the letters flawless in size and proportion. Noting this, my father once asked Oeroeg if he ever thought about his future.

'You could become an office clerk,' he added pensively, leafing through the exercises once more.

Oeroeg smiled and looked away with half-closed eyes, which he often did when at a loss for an answer.

'Oeroeg and I want to be train drivers, or pilots,' I said hastily. 'But most of all we want to be explorers. We both do.'

My father laid the exercise book aside with a hardly noticeable shrug of his shoulders. This was probably not the first time he had realised that an adult conversation with us was not on the cards. His attitude towards children in general was uneasy, to say the least. And so we lived our separate lives, side by side, speaking different languages.

Nevertheless, I know that my father was concerned about my education. A few days before my eleventh birthday he came to my room as I was getting ready for bed. He watched me as I hung my clothes over the back of a chair and brushed my teeth. I was reminded of a similar visit from my mother, years before, when she came to tell me that I would be going to school.

'You might want to make a list of presents you would like for your birthday,' my father began.

I nodded. I wanted to ask for rifles for Oeroeg and me, which we could take on our hunting expeditions, but I very much doubted my father would appreciate the necessity of such a gift.

'In a few months I shall be going on leave,' my father went on. 'I intend to do some travelling, see a bit of the world while I can still afford it. You realise that I can't take you along. I have been thinking of sending you to Holland, to boarding school maybe. At the end of this course you will be taking your entrance exam, and the next step will be the European High School. And life here . . .' He waved his hand dismissively. 'You are missing out on a lot, over here. You're going altogether native, and that bothers me.'

Standing by the washbasin, I braced myself and burst out: 'I don't want to go to Holland!' Gerard's stories flashed through my mind: rain and cold, stuffy rooms, boring city streets. 'I want to stay here,' I cried, 'and Oeroeg—'

My father interrupted me with an impatient gesture. 'Oeroeg, Oeroeg,' he said. 'It's always Oeroeg. You'll have to do without him some day. The pair of you have been friends for long enough. Don't you go around with the boys at your school? Why don't you invite a couple to join you here for your birthday? They can be picked up and driven back again in our car. I realise you have become attached to Oeroeg,' he added, noting my expression. 'It couldn't be helped. I had to do something for the boy, after all. But Oeroeg will be starting work when he leaves primary school, whereas you will be continuing your education. Besides . . .' He hesitated a moment. 'You do surely understand, don't you, my boy? You're European, remember.'

I thought about this, but the importance of being European was lost on me. At the insistence of my father I invited two classmates to spend the Sunday after my birthday at the plantation. My birthday presents did not include the rifles. I did get a stamp album, however, and a paintbox, which I promptly passed on, in secret, to Oeroeg. Gerard brought me the skin of a flying squirrel, properly cured, to hang on my wall. In addition, he decorated the back veranda with lanterns and coloured paper streamers, which added a festive touch to the somewhat forced birthday atmosphere.

My two guests, whom I barely knew other than as part of the boisterous crowd in the school playground, inspected my room and my possessions. Then they sat down with me and my father to a *rijsttafel* meal, which was a little more elaborate than normal for the occasion. Oeroeg had not been invited, and I was angry and disappointed, the more so since I had spoken to him about it, taking it for granted that he would be eating with us. Oeroeg did not seem to mind. From my seat I could see him in the garden, watching us. After the meal my father gave me and the two boys a tour of the factory, where he explained in detail how everything worked.

Later in the afternoon we were sent into the garden to amuse ourselves. Oeroeg joined us. It was then that I became aware, for the first time ever, of Oeroeg being regarded as a 'native' – not as an aristocratic native like my classmate Harsono Koesoma Soedjana, whose father was a regent, but as a *desa* boy, the son of a plantation worker. The difference lay in the slightly commanding tone my guests used towards Oeroeg, and in the bossy term 'Ajó!' telling him to hurry up with whatever game it was we were playing. I flushed with mortification, but the cause of it appeared to go unnoticed by Oeroeg. Only once did I see his sidelong, secret glance, and an almost imperceptible stiffening of his face and posture, when one of the boys, probably more in fun than with any evil intent, addressed him with an ugly Soendanese term of abuse.

After this incident Oeroeg kept his distance, contenting himself with sitting on the balustrade of the back veranda and watching us from there for the rest of the afternoon. That evening, when I returned from accompanying the boys to their homes in the car, Oeroeg was nowhere to be seen. It was the first time I had no idea where he was, or what he was doing. I went over to the pavilion, and found Gerard sitting on the porch with his long legs up on the table, smoking his pipe. I settled myself in a chair. Some minutes went by without either of us saying a word. Gerard was a master of the tactful, expectant silence when he surmised that confidences were about to be aired.

'Is Oeroeg any less than us?' I burst out finally. 'Is he any different?'

'That's rubbish,' Gerard said calmly, without removing the pipe from his mouth. 'Who said that?'

Haltingly, I gave account of the afternoon's events.

'A panther isn't the same as a monkey,' Gerard said after a pause. 'But is either one less than the other? A stupid question, you'll say, and rightly so. The same applies to human beings. Being different – that's normal.

Everybody's a little different from everybody else. I'm not the same as you. As for being less or more important on account of the colour of your skin or who your father is – that's nonsense. Oeroeg is your friend, isn't he? And if you can be friends with him, how can he possibly be *less* than you or anybody else?'

Making my way back to the house in the dark, I heard Oeroeg's voice coming from behind the servants' quarters. The houseboy, the gardener and Oeroeg were sitting on the low wall surrounding the well, discussing the cock Danoeh had bought the day before. I wanted to go over to them, but changed my mind. Instead I fetched my new paintbox from the back veranda, and took it to the cubicle by the kitchen where Oeroeg slept. A mosquito net hung limply from a wire above the wooden bunk. Oeroeg's school books lay in a neat pile on top of an over-turned crate. The whitewashed wall was decorated with pictures of planes and racing cars cut out of magazines. I knew he was very proud of his bare, orderly little room, which was never entirely free of pungent cooking smells, and where, especially at night, a damp chill rose from the cement floor. I left the paintbox on the bunk, next to an old pair of pyjamas, which, like most of my cast-offs, had found their way via the *baboe* to Oeroeg.

My father decided that I was to stay in the Indies, at any rate until my entrance exam. Since his replacement was to be quartered in the manager's house efforts were made to find accommodation for me in Soekaboemi. I knew very little of all this. My father confronted me with a fait accompli. He took me with him in the car to Soekaboemi, where he stopped in front of the house of the person whom I shall call Lida for the rest of my days.

Lida was a woman of indeterminate years. With hindsight, I take her to have been between thirty and forty at the time. She was one of those women whose appearance remains constant from adulthood to middle age and beyond. She was of medium height, rather thin and wore her pale blond hair in a short bob with a straight fringe covering her forehead. Her eyes were grey, and her features unremarkable, if a little irregular. She had come over from Holland as a nurse fairly recently, with the intention of setting up a rest home in the cool upland climate of Soekaboemi. However, the friend and colleague she had been counting on to join her in this venture had rushed headlong into marriage scarcely two months after arriving in the tropics, leaving Lida bereft of both assistance and capital. The big hotels and lodging houses springing up like mushrooms all over Soekaboemi offered fierce competition, and all that remained of her grand scheme was a small property with room for only a few lodgers. Lida could not afford to be choosy – her guest-house catered not only for people needing a rest, but also for holidaymakers and travellers requiring a bed for a few nights only. She even ran an informal restaurant, and had a reputation for being helpful and inexpensive – an amenable landlady. The headmaster of the European High School was an acquaintance of hers, and had recommended her to look after me for the duration of my father's furlough.

Lida's house had nothing of the Indies about it. It could just as well have been somewhere in Holland, in some leafy suburb like Laren or Blaricum. It had climbing plants over the gable and part of the roof, an adjoining conservatory and a garden full of roses. Cushions, doilies, tea cosies and hand-knotted rugs graced the interior, which seemed to have been designed with thoughts of a glowing fireplace in mind. I stared in wonder at the wainscoted walls, the cluttered rooms, the windows with net curtains as well as drapes.

Lida, who was expecting us, poured tea and came

straight to the point. I could tell that she and my father had met before, and that they had come to some sort of agreement. I learned that I would soon be moving in with Lida, and was so overcome by her resolute tone of voice and the suddenness of it all that at first I had neither the chance nor the desire to say what I was thinking.

'But . . . what about Oeroeg?' I stammered finally, during a lull in the conversation. 'What will Oeroeg do if I have to come and live here?'

Lida peered at me with her kindly, slightly short-sighted eyes. 'And who may Oeroeg be?' she asked, and when my father impatiently made to reply she quickly interposed: 'No, you tell me. Let him tell me himself.'

I stumbled over my words, because how could I possibly explain in a few sentences who Oeroeg was and what he meant to me? Oeroeg was my friend, practically my sole companion since birth, the only living soul with whom I had shared every phase of my existence, every thought, every experience. But he was more than that. To me Oeroeg signified life in and around Kebon Djati; he signified our mountain forays, the games we played in the tea gardens and on the stones in the river, our train rides to school – the alphabet of my childhood.

My father explained briefly that Oeroeg would be

staying on at the estate. 'He can go to the station on foot – it's not that far,' he declared. 'Or else we'll find another solution. Nothing for you to worry about.'

I began to suspect, not without reason, that my father thought going to live with Lida would wean me off my friendship with Oeroeg. The unfairness of it all filled me with anger and resentment, and for the remainder of my time on the estate I kept out of my father's way as much as possible.

I was playing truant more and more frequently, and the headmaster complained to Lida. Her reaction was to suggest that Oeroeg, who was equally to blame, should come and live with her. Oeroeg and I were almost twelve now, an age when any injustice meted out by adults, whether imagined or real, was likely to provoke open insubordination or furtive rebellion. We stayed away from school for hours, initially just to wander the streets and share news about our changed lives, but once in our stride either just Oeroeg and I, or a motley group of us half-grown boys, began to cause mischief in the *pasar* and the shops nearby. Oeroeg, in many ways more mature than me, as I came to realise later, rarely if ever seemed shocked by the initiations we received into aspects of life that we had never before encountered. There was Jules, a half-caste boy of about fifteen with a face disfigured by smallpox, who was the son of a prostitute frequented by the employees of plantations in the vicinity. They lived in a small house on a noisy, squalid lane, more like an alley-way, on the outskirts of the kampong. One day Jules took us there for a taste of *ketan*, a sweetmeat made with rice, grated coconut and brown sugar. Sonia, as she insisted we call her, was sitting on the steps of the back veranda in a stained pink kimono and bare feet. The tiny yard was littered with rubbish and broken bottles. Jules displayed not the slightest embarrassment when he showed us the shabby little bedroom festooned with cheap trinkets and paper flowers, and was quite forthcoming about the life led by his mother. I tried hard to act unimpressed, like Oeroeg, but with little success. All these new experiences left me in a turmoil of emotions, for which I found an outlet in unruly behaviour at school and moodiness at Lida's.

Even more disreputable than Jules was Adi, a nimble native lad whose skill at petty thieving was almost profes-sional. It was through him that we found ourselves for the first time at the cinema: a shed with wooden benches where old cowboy and gangster films were shown. The relentless succession of robberies, chases and murders made a huge impression on us, and we became so captivated by the cinema that we stopped at nothing to gain access to it.

It was at this stage that Lida, who was only half aware of what we were getting up to, decided to step in. Lida was a woman who did not beat about the bush. She possessed what Oeroeg and I in later years would call a 'soap-and-water' mentality: no imagination, no understanding of or belief in the existence of things she had no conception of and an overriding naivety which caused her one misfortune after another. She was bourgeois without being narrow-minded, and she embraced the pursuit of goodness in the Christian sense without bigotry. She assessed everyone and everything by the standards of her own straightforward, down-to-earth spirit. This combination of personality traits was not without a certain attractiveness, thanks to a total lack of guile or malice. Needless to say, she was forever being taken advantage of in her dealings with the local population, particularly by servants and tradespeople. Her sense of loyalty and her attempts to resolve conflicts and misunderstandings by means of logical and patient argument merely aroused confusion and mistrust. Displays of authority for the sake of prestige were foreign to her nature. Owing to the complete absence of mutual understanding, even well-disposed servants were dishonest with her. This was obvious to all who came and went, but not to Lida.

From the very beginning Lida doted on Oeroeg. Perhaps it was his loneliness that appealed to her maternal instinct, or maybe it was her strong though unconscious fondness for the exotic, since it was that interest which had doubtless moved her to come out to the Indies in the first place, but which now, in her new reduced circumstances, remained unfulfilled. It is also possible that Oeroeg's development from simple *desa* child to promising schoolboy reminded her of her own childhood and the difficulties she herself had faced when breaking free from a small-minded, uneducated milieu. Oeroeg was slim, well-proportioned and muscular, unlike me. I had the gawkiness of a boy who would likely grow tall, which indeed proved to be the case. Oeroeg's graceful build, his large eyes with pupils like inky mirrors floating in the bluish whites, his sharply outlined eyelids like those of a *wayang* puppet, his wide, well-defined mouth – his whole demeanour of ironic reserve with a touch of bashfulness – endeared him to Lida. Oeroeg's visits turned into overnight stays, and after a few months he became a permanent lodger at her house. He had every reason to prefer living there. The staff at Kebon Djati were now under the strict discipline of the temporary manager's wife. She regarded Oeroeg as a mere relative of the houseboy, and had turned him out of his little bedroom next to the kitchen to make him sleep in Danoeh's room behind the old stables. His clothes – mine before I outgrew them – were dirty and threadbare, and his hair had not been cut for a long time. He made a neglected impression.

'Since your father is paying for the boy's schooling what he now needs is a roof over his head,' Lida said in explanation of her decision to take Oeroeg under her wing.

An extra bed was put in my room, and an extra chair pulled up at the table. The few paying guests Lida had at that time took their meals in their rooms. And so Oeroeg became part of my daily life once more, this time as housemate as well as playmate.

I was aware that Lida corresponded with my father, and assumed that Oeroeg's presence in her home as well as his future came up for discussion. Now and then snippets of their exchanges trickled down to us. Lida's enquiries at the Dutch Native School revealed that Oeroeg was one of the brightest pupils. He was quick on the uptake, and showed a dedication to his studies that remained unaffected despite the occasional bout of restiveness. My father's plans to find Oeroeg an office job on the plantation after his seven years of primary education were known to the headmaster, who, however, believed that better things were reserved for a boy of Oeroeg's abilities, and advised that he should go on to secondary school. Lida was delighted to hear this, and promptly informed my father. His response, however, was unenthusiastic: all he could see was considerable expense with relatively little return, given the limited professional prospects for a boy of Oeroeg's background.

During the afternoons and evenings that Lida sat with us as we did our homework an idea had nestled in her brain, and she could think of little else. I can still see her sitting there, forever pushing up the glasses she needed for sewing. Oeroeg and I, who were actually rather fond of her, used to exchange meaningful smiles about the careless way she lounged in the low cane chair, exposing to all and sundry the pink elastic garters holding up her stockings. She wore shapeless dresses with puff sleeves, made of the cheap flowered material that was on sale at every *pasar*. Little did we suspect what was going through her mind as she sewed buttons on our shirts and mended our trousers; how, in those quiet hours, a plan was taking shape whose execution was to compensate her for her failed rest-home scheme. She would do everything in her power to help Oeroeg get ahead – he had to be given the opportunity of a good education – and she set about achieving her ambition with rigour. We always spoke Dutch in Lida's presence, on account of her poor knowledge of Malay and Soendanese. Oeroeg had to a certain extent overcome his earlier shyness, but was still more inclined to listen than talk. Now Lida energetically took him in hand, meaning to improve his pronunciation. Not a day went by without her holding forth on the merits of the medical profession, about the great need there was for medical care for people in the tropics. She quoted facts and figures on epidemics and brought home books and brochures for us, but especially for Oeroeg. She raked up the lessons she had learned during her own training as a nurse, showing us illustrations of the interior structure of the human body with the different organs, the tracery of arteries and the location of muscles. At first we looked and listened with more politeness than interest, and I was quite surprised one day to hear Oeroeg reply 'perhaps' to

Lida's question whether he would like to become a doctor, and even more so when, shortly after that, his answer was a straightforward 'yes, I would'.

That night in our room I accused Oeroeg of betraying our ambition to become pilots.

'So what?' said Oeroeg. 'If that's what she wants.'

'What do you think of Lida?' I asked. This was the first time it occurred to me that our feelings towards the woman taking care of us might be open to question.

Oeroeg gave me one of his dark sidelong looks before replying.

'She's alright,' he said finally.

Then, with a wild grimace, he launched into a highly realistic imitation of Lida bargaining with a Chinese *klontong*, which sent both of us rolling over our beds in hysterics until the people in the next room banged on the wall and Lida came running to tell us to pipe down.

My entrance exam coincided roughly with my father's return. I had not seen him for over a year. He had put on some weight and sported a tan, which, together with his well-cut Palm Beach suit, gave him the look of a traditional gentleman planter at last. I was taken aback by his boisterous high spirits, and by his generosity with gifts from overseas, but most astonishing of all was that he had brought back a new wife with him. There had been no hint of this in his letters. They had married in Singapore, and she was staying on in Batavia for the moment to do some shopping.

Lida refrained from making any comment, but it was obvious that she took a dim view of my father's actions. Oeroeg was transferred from one guardian to another without any deliberation, and it was decided that I should spend the long holidays at the plantation. No further mention was made by my father of any plans to send me to school in Holland, presumably because of the cost. At least that was what I thought when I got to know my stepmother, who abhorred unnecessary expense. She was a fresh, practical, down-to-earth young woman, with a pretty but somewhat expressionless face. I took an instant dislike to her, due to her imperious reorganization of the Kebon Djati household and her haughty way with the domestic servants as well as with the estate's employees. As a governess and schoolteacher she had spent some years in a position of comparative subordination, and now seemed determined to make up for it as the manager's wife. At home she was indisputably the one in charge. My father greatly admired her efficiency, and was visibly charmed by her health and vigour. In contrast to my mother, who had always risen late and seldom exchanged her negligee for proper daywear, Eugenie joined my father at the breakfast table neatly dressed and with the housekeeping activities well under way.

I escaped whenever I could from the new atmosphere pervading the house. Usually I went to see Oeroeg in Soeka-boemi, but sometimes we would escape to the countryside to explore or go swimming in one of the mountain pools. Lida had taken over a guesthouse in Batavia, where she and Oeroeg would be going to live in September. Oeroeg would be attending secondary school there, after which he would go on to study at the Netherlands-Indies Medical College in Soerabaja. Lida had the whole plan worked out.

We also paid a visit to Sidris, who found little to say to her son. The expression on her care-worn face was a mixture of pride and bewilderment as she slowly shook her head, only dimly aware of what the future held. Over the years her home had lost every trace of Western comfort. A few grimy mats served as seats in the dilapi-dated front porch, there was rubbish heaped up in the yard, and everywhere the stench of dried fish and *trasih*.

Satih, now definitely running to fat, sat in the doorway in a sarong and tight bodice, winding her gleaming hair into a knot. She had no intention of staying in the *desa*, she told us. Instead she wanted to go to the city and work as a *baboe*.

Oeroeg and I sat on our heels with Sidris and the children, feeling slightly out of place there for the first time in our lives. The year of order and regularity in Lida's spotless home had awakened in us a consciousness of the squalor and poverty of village life. Beside his unkempt brothers and sisters Oeroeg looked princely. We all ate together: rice and a sort of crisp made from dried, ground prawns. Oeroeg said goodbye to his family, and we set off back.

It was the hottest time of day, and we went down the stony lane at a leisurely pace. Large, frothy clouds, sliced off underneath as though resting on a ledge of glass, drifted across the glaring afternoon sky. The green carpet on the mountain slopes glistened in the light. The air was filled with the lethargic stillness of the sweltering heat of day. Only the faint barking of a dog and the distant tinkle of water-buffalo bells reached us over the fields. There was not a soul to be seen on the road or in the *sawahs*, nor were there any brightly coloured tea pickers' headscarves dotted about the greenery of the tea gardens higher up the mountain. Lining the road were *tambleang* bushes with blooms in every shade of pink, red and orange, all swarming with butterflies. The river, half-hidden by the lush vegetation on its banks, splashed invitingly as it flowed around the boulders on its bed.

Oeroeg suggested going for a swim. We threw our clothes in a heap on the ground and waded into the fresh, crystal-clear water. Proper swimming was not possible in the shallow pools, so we kept plunging in full-length, or leaning back into the foaming water cascading down the stepped rock formations. We had done this hundreds of times when we were small and both living at Kebon Djati. The unconditional surrender to the bubbling, clattering water, the plunging and frolicking, all the games we played in the river – they were among the most intense experiences of our childhood. This time, however, Oeroeg and I felt a twinge of disappointment. Bathing in the river had lost its blissfulness. Perhaps that is putting it too strongly, better to say that from that moment on bathing in the river would be no more than a refreshing dip, an activity arising from an all-absorbing craving to cool off, which, once satisfied, left little reason to linger in the water.

We continued splashing about for some time, out of habit, and likely out of a sense of awkwardness too, but without anything like our old jollity. The difference was that we now saw it all – the bathing, the rocks in the river, the sparkling current – with different eyes, eyes that had lost the ability to see the real world as a world of wonder. Gone was the magical kingdom in which we were the heroes and explorers. The mysterious grottos were nothing but deep shadows beneath overhanging foliage, our old hunting-ground of rocky plateaus and unbridge-able rapids only a mountain stream coursing over its bed of gravel and jutting stones. Crabs and dragonflies, a-shimmer with alluring colours, shot away under and over the surface, but they no longer took our breath away, for all that we made to chase them in the old spirit of rivalry. As we lay on our backs to dry on a slab of rock, the true significance of these changes flashed through my mind. I glanced at Oeroeg, and saw the same discovery in his eyes. A sense of finality. We were children no longer.

Eugenie was pregnant. As a consequence of this I had no trouble persuading my father to let me go to the European High School in Batavia. Indeed, I had the impression that my wish came as an unexpected solution to a delicate problem. Lodging with Lida as before was out of the question, however – I was to be a boarder at the school. I left for Batavia shortly before the school year began. Oeroeg and Lida had departed a few weeks earlier. The city was new to me, and I was overwhelmed by the vast squares, the imposing white mansions and the busy traffic.

The school boarding-house, an old-fashioned building with sombre rooms and tiled floors, stood among other large mansions on a stretch of land with parched grass along the road. A pair of towering succulents with spiky, leathery leaves stood like sentries on either side of the entrance. The establishment was run by a married couple, with the husband, a teacher, supervising the boys' schoolwork and the wife acting as housemistress. The appearance of the place was clearly ruled by considerations of order and efficiency, with furniture and decoration kept to a minimum. The high-ceilinged bedrooms with whitewashed walls and bare floorboards accommodated four pupils each, and were accordingly furnished with four beds, four lockers, four chairs and four coat pegs. In this setting the beds with their boxy, starched mosquito nets reminded me more than ever of cages. There were bars on the windows, to protect against burglary, so I was informed. Sharing this room with me were three older boys who took little notice of me, aside from borrowing my pencils and tearing pages out of my exercise books to scribble on.

The daily timetable was simple. After breakfast at seven o'clock we went to our classrooms via the back yard adjoining the school garden. We returned at one o'clock. Lunch was served on three or four long tables on the back veranda. We ate largely in silence, as conversation was against the rules. From two to half past three we had to rest, which meant keeping absolutely quiet. We would read, take a nap, or do homework, the latter in the hope of being exempted from working under supervision later on, which all of us loathed. Homework was normally done in the inside gallery, forbiddingly furnished with rows of old school desks. That was where we went after tea, to labour over our grammars and sums, if necessary until dinnertime. But once you had finished your homework, and provided the supervisor was satisfied, you were free until eight.

Unsurprisingly, the strict discipline we were subjected to was not conducive to a congenial atmosphere. Pent-up feelings vented themselves in sudden outbursts of rowdiness and bad language. On the whole there was very little true friendship between the boys. There would be temporary alliances lasting for the duration of a term, but that was all. With the exception of a few, I did not much like my fellow boarders. I did join in with their pranks at times, and also with the secret smutty talk, but for the rest their games left me cold.

If I finished my homework early I would go and see Oeroeg at Lida's, which was also where I spent the greater part of my Sundays. The guesthouse Lida now kept was situated nearby, in an untidy neighbourhood that had seen a considerable decline in recent years. The houses, occupied by Chinese and Indo families, were poorly maintained. Small shops and foodstalls had sprung up between the larger dwellings, so that the kampong at the back of the gardens appeared to be spilling down towards the street. It seemed that Lida, who lacked a discriminating eye in these matters, had put a millstone around her neck by exchanging her former establishment for this one. While her garden was reasonably tidy and her front porch freshly whitened, the location worked against her. Even the proud sign by the gate bearing the name in Dutch was overshadowed. She had a handful of lodgers: a few bachelors working in downtown offices, who were seldom home except for the evening meal; an elderly couple; who had known better days 'in sugar' and who, since the depression, had become steadily more impoverished; and two young women whose morals were above suspicion to Lida, but not to Oeroeg and me. She had a cheeky house-boy and three rather slovenly *baboes* to assist her in meeting the needs of her paying guests, who occupied identically furnished rooms, each with its own veranda and chairs.

The fuss and bother of life in Batavia did not agree with Lida, nor did the heat. She was less bright and cheer-ful than she had been in Soekaboemi, and had hardly any time for us. She was usually to be found in her office – a small, stuffy room in one of the outbuildings – with a pile of bills in front of her, her fringe stuck to her damp fore-head and her flowered dress stained round the collar. When I dropped by to see Oeroeg in the afternoons, she would greet me absentmindedly and send us to the kitchen to ask for lemonade or tea. No expense or effort was spared on behalf of Oeroeg. He always looked as neat as a new pin in white polo shirt and linen shoes. He no longer wore his Muslim hat. When I asked him about this, he waved his hand dismissively, clacking his tongue. 'I'm not a Muslim,' he said. It was true that I had never seen him show much interest in his religion, although I did remember him going to the mosque with our house-boy at Kebon Djati.

Bareheaded, he seemed to look less like himself. The European clothes and modern cut of his thick hair detracted from his distinctive air of modesty and reserve, which I had always taken to be an innate quality of his. Oeroeg said he liked his school, a Dutch Native institution with pupils hailing from a variety of backgrounds. He was among those at the top of his class. He had adopted the mannerisms and speech of the half-caste youths roaming the streets on their brightly painted racing bikes, flamboyantly dressed in imitation of film stars and sports heroes. He had also started smoking, to which Lida turned a blind eye. She was proud of her foster son, and did all she could for him. She and Oeroeg each had a bedroom in the outbuilding, but his was larger and better furnished than hers.

Lida's main source of displeasure was the condescending, derisive attitude taken by her lodgers towards her and Oeroeg – even she couldn't help noticing it, although she was too naive to grasp the deeper implications of their gossip. Oeroeg was well aware of this, but seemed to find it quite amusing much of the time. He paid little attention to the bachelors, treated the elderly couple with downright arrogance, and as to the two young women, I had never known him to behave with more brazen effrontery than he did in their presence. When we went into the garden in the afternoon, they would usually be sitting out on their small veranda in their loose kimonos, doing their nails or some such. With their hair undone and their feet in worn slippers propped up on the balustrade, they would tip their cane chairs back and forth in a most free and easy manner, calling out to us and making saucy remarks, the double meaning of which often didn't catch up with me until later.

Oeroeg just smiled his secret smile and glanced away, as though to hide his embarrassment. Yet we kept hovering nearby, which often resulted in their bringing out jars of candied tamarind and *goelali*, so that Oeroeg and I would end up perched on the balustrade of their veranda savouring their sweets while the banter became ever racier. Oeroeg could say the rudest things with a half-smile while looking the girls straight in the eye, at which they became quite flustered, not knowing whether to take offence or not. Their usual response was a playful slap across the face or kick to the shins, challenging him to a romp. Although I knew that I was supposed to disapprove of these girls their conversations and their teasing manner fascinated me. I felt guilty hearing Lida call me from the house to say it was time for me to go back to the school boarding-house, and was completely overwhelmed by Oeroeg's cool self-confidence as he delivered a parting sneer to the girls and casually lit a cigarette before walking a short way back with me.

I did not seem to have as much affinity with him as in the early days. The problems of puberty that I was coping with seemed not to affect him at all. Next to him I felt childish and ignorant, a sense of inferiority that was probably exacerbated by my restricted freedom of movement. Oeroeg could do what he liked in the evenings, while I was hardly ever permitted to go into town after nine o'clock.

I do not know what inspired Lida to devote herself so entirely to Oeroeg. I can only guess. I am describing the events as I experienced them at the time. Never again will the opportunity arise for me to ask the people concerned to explain what they once said and did. I am still in the dark as to her motives. Sometimes I think it was because of her own loneliness that she took charge of Oeroeg, a deep-seated need to find among her fellow human beings one person on whom she could lavish affection and care.

She had trained as a nurse, after all, a profession that tends to reflect unfulfilled maternal instincts in those who choose it. Sometimes too I had the feeling that it was all Oeroeg's doing, that he had cast a spell on her, and on me and on everybody else, that he was in possession of one of those strangely passive personalities that exert an irresistible attraction.

During his secondary school years in Batavia he shed all the habits that had marked him as a boy from the *desa* back in Soekaboemi. Indeed, I had the impression he was doing this deliberately to blot out the past. He only spoke Dutch now, and wore conspicuously European clothes. He was never on familiar terms with Lida's servants, and tried to ignore allusions to our childhood or to Sidris and his brothers and sisters. The only time he almost punched me was when I mentioned his father in the presence of some of his schoolmates. Much to my surprise I began to notice that Oeroeg wanted to pass for a half-caste. Until then I had only known him to show a certain dislike or even disdain for the Eurasian community. His wish to assimilate with the European world was evidently so strong as to warrant making this concession. The transition from the old ways to the new was facilitated as much by living at Lida's as by his close association with his schoolmates, of whom at least three quarters were of mixed ancestry and like him eager to Europeanise. One day I came upon Oeroeg and Lida discussing the possibility of his taking Lida's surname. I even remember Lida trying to address Oeroeg as Ed or Ted or suchlike for a while, but she couldn't keep it up.

Oeroeg and I went to the cinema together from time to time, but usually he went alone. Our interest had now shifted from cowboys and Indians to Tarzan and horror films, and we took to defying the age restriction on films of love and passion. After the cinema, where we usually fell in with some of Oeroeg's friends, we went to a Chinese café that was modelled in both service and appearance on the typical American drugstore. Surrounded by nickel and glass we sat on our bar stools savouring our ices or *bami* to the accompaniment of jazz music blaring from an electric gramophone. We now came into contact with girls too, mostly sisters of Oeroeg's friends: dark-haired, early-ripe types, whose giggles and sudden endearments threw me into confusion. Oeroeg's favourite among them was the fair-complexioned Poppie. It was at this girl's home that we learned to dance. We considered not being able to dance a tiresome deficiency in our education.

Poppie lived with her mother, a prodigiously fat Eurasian divorcee, in a new neighbourhood on the edge of town. The small, modern bungalow stood in a bare, sun-scorched yard where nothing seemed to want to grow. The heat in the living room, which had leaded windows, was unbearable. With our shirts sticking to our backs we led the girls round the room in tangos or waltzes, to the scratchy, plaintive tones of old gramophone records. Poppie's mother lounged back in her chair with a paper fan in her hand, watching us.

Our chief entertainment in those days consisted of dancing and going to the cinema, but on Sundays we sometimes made expeditions to the harbour or the tidal mangrove forest outside Tandjoeng Priok. We roamed the strong-smelling fish market, watched the proas with their reddish-brown sails glide along the canal and walked all the way to the lighthouse at the end of the narrow pier, where the crumbling cement blocks were overgrown with algae and slithery shells, and where even the sea breeze brought no relief from the heat. The white-hot light shimmered above the corrugated zinc roofs of the harbour sheds, above the grit-covered docksides and the white buildings around the fish market. A haze of vapour drifted over the sea, blurring the horizon. Sometimes we swam out some way from the pier, chiefly to show how daring we were, since we knew there were sharks in the area.

Even more alluring to us were the tidal mangrove forests, in spite of the malarial mosquitoes swarming around the livid, naked stems at low tide. The ground underfoot was pulpy, and the air was filled with a briny odour of decay. Around the stems standing in water there was a continuous squelching sound coming from the roots, and the plop of air pockets rising to the surface of the thick mud marking the division between land and sea. Now and then we came to a small beach in a recess of the mangrove forest, but the water was not inviting, and besides, we would be attacked by mosquitoes the moment we stripped off our clothes. We usually walked some distance along the shore, in single file, stooping to avoid the tough branches blocking our path. If we found a patch of dry ground, we stopped for a rest.

Our conversations always revolved around the same topics: school, the friends we had in common, sport, films and girls. One day the question of our future came up. We were lying on our backs, knees raised, handkerchiefs under our heads. There were clouds of insects, which we tried to blow away with cigarette smoke. I told Oeroeg that I was planning to study engineering.

'And you?' I asked, after explaining my own choice at some length. 'Still planning to go to that medical college? Is that what you really want?'

Oeroeg flicked the stub of his cigarette into the bushes.

'Oh well, why not?' was his off-hand reply. 'Whatever. But an office job – no thanks. At least a doctor is his own boss. They'll come flocking to me for *potong*.' He made a guttural, throat-slitting sound by way of illustration.

'Your patients will be impressed,' I said. 'And scared of you too, I bet.'

'*Desa* folk, all of them,' muttered Oeroeg, lighting another cigarette. 'They all have their local *doekoens*, who do more harm than good with their traditional herbs and hocus-pocus, but they prefer that to seeing a proper doctor.'

'I know what you mean, but they'll have more confidence in you because you're . . .' I was going to say 'because you're one of them', but swallowed my words when Oeroeg flashed me a fiercely forbidding look from the corner of his eyes.

'So what will you do then?' I hurried on. 'Work for the government?' I remembered having heard something about scholarships being available for medical training in the Indies.

Oeroeg shrugged. He raised himself to sit on his haunches, and the ease with which he balanced his entire weight on the balls of his feet, with his shoulders, back and hips forming a perfectly relaxed curve, could not have been more revealing of his origins.

'Maybe,' he said guardedly. After a short pause he added: 'I'll be going away, though, for sure.'

I sat up. 'Where to? To Holland?' I asked.

Oeroeg made the two-toned throaty sound which, in the Indies, counts as an affirmative. 'I'd rather go to America, though,' he said abruptly.

He had made a little pile of pebbles and shells, and began to aim them one after another at a tree stump nearby. To his mind America was the land of promise, a land where, so we both imagined, everything was bigger, better and smarter than anywhere else in the world. Influenced by films and books we also thought of it as a place of extremes, where skyscrapers and technical miracles existed alongside the vast plains of the Wild West. But Oeroeg's desire was not only for adventure. I realised later that he believed – mistakenly, of course – that race and parentage would be of no account for him or anyone else in the New World.

We also talked about Lida. It was never quite clear to

me where Oeroeg stood in relation to her. Looking back I cannot say that he treated her with affection, or even with noticeable respect. He seemed to take it all for granted – the care she lavished on him, the sacrifices she made, her unflagging interest in his progress, her forgivingness and her complete confidence in him. As I have noted before, Oeroeg was a naturally passive creature. He accepted the course his life was taking, just as he had previously accepted his life at Kebon Djati and having me as his friend. I do not believe the relationship between him and Lida was ever really close. Oeroeg was quite tractable, and in general did as he was told without protest. Nor do I think Lida particularly wished there to be an emotional bond between them. She simply wanted to be a benign factor in the development of his life, which in all its forms of expression remained foreign to her, but which possibly appealed to her all the more for that. She herself was too modest, or too down-to-earth, either to show or to expect tenderness. I can well imagine that she felt amply rewarded by his excellent school reports, which reflected the successful transformation of a poor country lad into a clever secondary schoolboy. Besides, she was too busy working to pay much attention to him.

Running her new guesthouse was by no means plain

sailing for Lida. It grieves me to think how hard she had to struggle in an environment that was hostile to her nature and habit. When Oeroeg was fifteen – he was in his second year – she discovered by chance that his afternoon visits to the aforementioned young women staying on her premises, supposedly to get sweets or to run small errands for them, were not entirely innocent. I heard from Oeroeg afterwards how it had all come about. Suffice it to say that Lida was greatly perturbed. She realised for the first time that this was an area in which Oeroeg needed guidance. Typically, she refused to believe Oeroeg was in any way at fault, and gave the young women notice to leave, turning a deaf ear to their protestations of being falsely accused. She blamed herself for having allowed such a situation to arise under her own roof, the more so for not having noticed anything earlier. Regarding this new aspect of Oeroeg's education she was at a loss. She began to keep a close eye on him, and also saw danger where there was none. The forays into town with his friends, the dancing lessons at Poppie's house, the visits to the cinema, all these things made her sick with worry. She knew Oeroeg well enough to realise that it was not the biological facts that he needed instruction in, but the savoir-faire that would enable him to distinguish between common decency and coarseness, honour and dishonour, self-restraint and self-will. Lida felt it was a man's job to initiate him in these matters. She suddenly foresaw complications and conflicts if Oeroeg were to pass the turbulent years of his adolescence with her at the guesthouse. It was not that she feared a repetition of the incident with the young women. Rather, she doubted her ability to enforce the necessary discipline. The obvious thing for her to do was to appeal to the only person of authority she was acquainted with in Batavia: the headmaster of my school. I do not know how Lida managed to persuade him to find a place in the school boarding-house for a boy of Oeroeg's background and education. Presumably, financial considerations came into play, rather than idealism, but it is also possible that he had simply taken a liking to Lida.

Oeroeg was quartered at the boarding-house until the end of his course. At first he felt hurt and offended at being put under restraint. The strict daily schedule was loathsome to him, as was the general atmosphere of the place. He became insolent and disorderly, broke the rules about leaving the premises and cut himself off from me as well. Gradually I came to realise that his rebellious behaviour had less to do with wanting more freedom than with wanting to impress the other boys, in the belief that the only way of winning their sympathy would be by acting the devil-may-care bad boy. It was common knowledge that Oeroeg and I were friends, and had been since before he became a boarder like the rest of us. I had never made a secret of where he came from – the opinions of the other boys, in so far as they were critical or derisive, had never worried me anyway. Nor had I been bothered by comments like 'Oh, we saw you at the *pasar* with your *djongos*,' or 'Been out with your native chum again, have you?' because I knew they were just teasing, and it did not affect my relationship with them at all. But this changed when Oeroeg moved in. Before long the pair of us were to some degree isolated from the others. Not that there was anything remotely resembling a boycott. Indeed, I am convinced the majority of them were unaware of anything out of the ordinary. To what extent Oeroeg's defiance played a part I cannot tell, although a mischief-maker was obviously more likely to be admired than disliked by the boarders. What set us apart was Oeroeg's indefinable 'otherness', the subtle difference in his behaviour and mentality, in his 'aura' I would say if it were possible to put these things into words.

There was no question of hostility towards Oeroeg. It

was more like indifference. His efforts to draw attention to himself failed to rouse the desired interest in him, as I believe he quite soon came to realise. He continued to show off for a while, but then suddenly lapsed into a state of withdrawal such as I had never seen in him, even at Kebon Djati. He became taciturn, and the dark, guarded look never left his eyes. We slept in the same room, but the presence of the two other boys gave us little opportunity for private conversation. Besides, I doubt Oeroeg would have confided in me anyway. We hardly ever went out for a walk together now, and even when we did he carefully kept me at a distance. I had known Oeroeg for too long to be upset by this. I was in the throes of puberty myself – with just as little guidance as him at the time – and I could sense, not without sympathy, what Oeroeg was going through. Maintaining a sense of equality was easy enough at his day school, but it was not so at the boarding-house. Neither clothing nor behaviour could give him what he wanted: to be one of us.

It was probably around this time too that Oeroeg and I began to drift apart. Oeroeg could not help identifying me with the other European boys, by whom he felt rejected. I knew that he had stopped seeing his half-caste mates after school, and had taken up with a certain

Abdullah Haroedin, a boy of mixed Arab ancestry who, like him, planned to go to the medical college. I felt excluded, and even rather jealous. Whether this was down to Oeroeg himself or to Abdullah I am not sure. In any case we rarely if ever formed a threesome. In retrospect, I am inclined to think that his friendship with Abdullah provided a welcome alternative to the situation he found himself in at the boarding-house. Abdullah was short and plump, with an intelligent look about him, and frizzy hair. He wore large, black-framed glasses, which gave him a slightly comic appearance. His sense of humour was very similar to Oeroeg's – they shared a world of ideas from which I felt increasingly removed as I grew older. It happened frequently that Oeroeg and I did not go over to Lida's on Sundays or free evenings because he had already promised to meet Abdullah. I was disappointed by this, and one day I told Oeroeg as much. He just stared at me in silence, and I even thought I detected a certain satisfaction in his eyes. Heart-to-heart talk was out of the question now.

In the school holidays I spent some time at Kebon Djati, which I found utterly transformed, as though by magic. The house was filled with new furniture, the garden freshly laid out with gravel paths and well-tended flowerbeds. There was not a single servant I recognised from the old days. Eugenie's figure had become more rounded, and she had an air of almost overbearing robustness. It was she who ruled the roost, not only in the manager's private quarters, but by all accounts in the rest of the estate as well. As for my father, he seemed healthy and content. He had acquired a double chin that bulged over his shirt collar, which, oddly enough, made him resemble those large frogs Oeroeg and I used to catch when we were children. Seeing him sprawled in his armchair with his shirtsleeves rolled up and the belt of his trousers stretched tight over his paunch, I could barely imagine him being the same person who used to sit in the inner gallery listening to scratchy gramophone records with a doleful expression on his face. The gramophone had gone, and in its place stood my stepbrother's playpen. One time my father gave me some letters my mother had written from Nice, where she now lived, apparently. I shrank from the mauve, faintly scented notepaper. My mother's tone was that of someone addressing a young child, and she had enclosed a picture of a new racing car model cut out of a magazine. I noticed Eugenie looking at it, and the blood rushed to my cheeks. My mother also sent her regards to Oeroeg, asking 'What has become of him?' I stored the letters away in the guest-room wardrobe, and decided not to answer them. Gerard was on leave at the time, so my loneliness at Kebon Djati was complete.

I wandered aimlessly in the tea gardens, the only part of the estate that was unchanged. The bitter fragrance of clipped leaves, the flowers of the flame trees against the sky, the tea pickers' voices faintly audible from afar in the stillness – it was all still the same enchanting place, where the passing of the years seemed irrelevant and as fleeting as a dream. I sat down on the grassy edge of a gulley and gazed out over the plain, which was overlaid with a bluish heat haze. I could hear the wind sighing in the bamboo thickets by the *desa* and the bubble of streamlets hidden in the green, I could see the clouds of butterflies over the *tambleang* bushes, but I was left feeling as though I couldn't take it all in. There was something deeply incongruous about being there without Oeroeg. It seemed to me that my senses were dulled by his absence, that the landscape was incomplete without him.

It was out of a desire to make up for this emptiness that I decided to pay Sidris a visit – but there too I had become a stranger. Sidris was reluctant to call me by my first name as she used to do in the old days, for I had grown too tall and manly in her eyes, nor did she wish me to squat down on the mat in her front porch. A rickety chair was duly fetched from the back, and there I sat, towering above Sidris and her companions, cringing with embarrassment. Sidris spoke to me using the Soendanese honorifics denoting an inferior addressing a superior. I dearly wanted to reply using the same polite forms, but did not dare in case she thought I was mocking her. Sidris asked after Oeroeg, whom she had not seen for more than two years. She spoke of him in a tone in which I thought I heard wistfulness as well as pride. There was no hint of criticism of his failure to come and visit her or keep in touch by letter. I had the impression that she had resigned herself to the fact that Oeroeg had left her and her world forever. I did not stay long with Sidris. Descending the footpath on my way back I felt as though the *sawahs*, the verdant slopes, the clouds gathering above the mountain ridges, the whole panorama was etching itself in my brain more sharply than ever before, as though a consciousness beyond my own knew that this was the last time I would see it all the way I saw it now.

I also went to Telaga Hideung. I had never been back since the accident. Strangely, even in broad daylight the lake seemed lit by the moon. The light shafting down through the trees and overhanging branches onto the water was greenish-gold, as though filtered through stained-glass windows. I saw the water plants, the circles and ripples on the surface where Oeroeg's father had vanished into the depths. All around me the forest lay in noonday stillness. Only the leaves at the very tops of the trees quivered in a faint breeze. I stared at the dark shadows among the green, where I used to think Nèneh Kombèl would be lurking. Although I had long since stopped believing in ghosts the sight of the lake still filled me with dread. I could not put a name to this fear, this indefinable sense of doom assailing me as I gazed at the greenish-black surface. I had the impression that the water was completely stagnant in certain parts of the lake, where the reflection of the trees was dull and lacking the inky translucence of the surrounding areas. I stared at those strange, clearly defined pools, and one time I thought I saw a reddish shimmer in the deep, like dark blood. A leaf fluttering down from a tree made me jump, with my heart pounding. The water was hostile, alien, an unknowable element. A cloud passed over the sun, and dusk fell on the lake. I turned and ran down the narrow path back to the road, stumbling over roots and stones. I had a sensation of something luring me to look back, but I forced myself not to. The next day I returned to Batavia.

Oeroeg had completed his course with flying colours, and had left for Soerabaja. I still had another two years of high school ahead of me. Writing letters was not Oeroeg's forte, as I might have expected. I had to content myself with the news passed on to me by Lida. I went to see her more often now, not so much to hear about Oeroeg as to find a glimmer of the warm domesticity I had known at her house in Soekaboemi, which was something entirely lacking at the boarding-house. But Lida had lost the ability to conjure up the cosy atmosphere of old. The tropical heat and her financial worries had made her nervous, and her experiences with lodgers and servants alike had finally undermined her trusting instincts. There was only an occasional flash of the old 'soap-and-water' mentality, which Oeroeg and I, despite our mockery, had always secretly valued. The more disillusioned she became with running her establishment, the greater her expectations with regard to Oeroeg. She showed me a picture of him posing among his classmates, mostly native students.

'He looks really fine, don't you think?' Lida asked,

peering at the photograph through her needlework glasses. 'He likes it there, which doesn't surprise me. He's such a quick learner. Soerabaja is a nice place, by the sound of it. He's living with Abdullah, at Abdullah's relatives'.'

An undertone of longing in her voice made me look up. Her face was thin, with jutting cheekbones, and her fringe, stuck to her moist forehead as usual, was turning grey. Suddenly I realised what she was hinting at. She wanted to go to Soerabaja. That I had guessed right became clear in the followings months. She took to discussing Oeroeg's letters at length with me. He seemed to be increasingly absorbed in his work, and had joined several organizations about which he gave no particulars, but which took up much of his time. The tone of the letters took me somewhat by surprise. It was hard for me to imagine them being written by Oeroeg – Oeroeg, the lover of the cinema and ice bars, the imitator of *Indo* dandies, the clever but disaffected schoolboy. There were passages in his letters from Soerabaja revealing a very different interest. He criticised the government regulations on medical practice and hygiene, giving examples of neglect with respect to native patients from the lower classes. The words he used sounded to me as if they were someone else's, not his own. He had nonetheless registered as a prospective Netherlands-Indies doctor, and was consequently entitled to a government grant. I happened to remark on this once to Lida.

'It's just as well he sees errors where errors are being made,' she said evasively.

There then followed a period during which the letters grew infrequent, and about those she received Lida was less forthcoming. She seemed distracted and irritable, weighed down by problems that confounded her. At long last she reached a conclusion: she would dispose of her guesthouse in Batavia, just as she had done in Soekaboemi. Soon afterwards she departed with a carload of suitcases and furniture to Soerabaja.

My contact with Oeroeg and Lida was reduced to sporadic letters, a postcard from time to time, or a hastily written note. From this correspondence I gathered that Lida too had been welcomed into the home of Abdullah's relatives. She was working as head nurse in a native hospital. Usually it was she who wrote to me, while Oeroeg sometimes merely scribbled his name or a greeting at the bottom of her letter.

The Black Lake

Time flew by for me, as I was studying hard for my final exams. I passed with reasonably good marks, as I expected after all the cramming I had done. My father came to Batavia, and we discussed my future. I was seventeen, going on eighteen, and tall for my age. The housemistress at school had seen to it that I was supplied with long trousers, as I had begun to present a ludicrous picture with my too-short shorts and long, hairy legs. Over a glass of beer at the Harmonie Club my father set out his plan. He was in agreement that I should study engineering, and had decided that I should go to Delft forthwith. From that day on everything moved apace. A passage was booked for me on a mail ship, and a new, freshly painted cabin trunk was provided for my few belongings. As Eugenie was about to give birth to a second child it was not convenient for me to stay at Kebon Djati while I waited for my sailing date. So before leaving for Holland I went to Soerabaja, to bid Oeroeg and Lida goodbye.

Oeroeg was waiting for me at the railway station. Like me he was in long, white trousers. His face was thinner than I remembered, and more sharply defined. I noticed almost at once that he was wearing his Muslim cap again. He stood motionless, leaning on one hip, hands on his waist, eyes fixed on the people passing through the ticket barrier. Catching sight of me he came forward to greet me unhurriedly, nonchalantly. For an instant he was a stranger to me. There was no trace of the loose-limbed lad with his American canvas shoes and brightly coloured polo shirts, with his *branie* ways and his rapid sidelong glances in which both shyness and veiled mockery could be read. Instead there stood before me an earnest-looking young man, more mature than I was, a native East Indian exuding a new air of comfortable self-confidence. I felt rather awkward at first. We chatted about our studies, my exams, his training. I asked about his friends, his pastimes.

'I spend quite a lot of time with . . .' he wavered a moment, 'with a set of like-minded people. There is so much to be done.'

I took this to be an allusion to the organizations he had mentioned in his letters, and said: 'I gather you've joined some clubs. What do you do there? Do you have a good time?'

'Oh, they're not social clubs,' Oeroeg replied hastily. 'You misunderstand me. We don't have much time for that kind of thing. Which is not to say we don't have a good time, though.'

'No more dancing then, I take it?' I asked, teasingly.

Oeroeg's eyes seemed to darken; he didn't even smile. 'There is so much to be done,' he repeated.

The rickshaw we had taken from the station halted in front of a traditional East Indies house in a quiet tree-lined street. The front veranda was barely visible behind a profusion of potted palms and lush maidenhair ferns ranged on the steps and balustrades. From the dim interior emerged a woman in a shapeless flowered-cotton dress and slippers, with grey hair smoothed back and fastened on either side with pins. There was something markedly East Indian about her gait. It was Lida.

'Hello,' she said, showing a trace of her former fresh smile. She brushed her hand across her brow and invited me to step inside.

In the back sat Abdullah and his relatives: a stout elderly figure in a pyjama suit, and two girls of about sixteen with delicate Javanese features. Abdullah's appearance was less changed than Oeroeg's. He greeted me warmly, and pulled up a rocking chair for me. The conversation was a little strained. Neither Oeroeg nor Lida nor I were able to retrieve the familiar tone of the old days. I had a sense that this would never be possible again. I barely recognised Lida – lounging back in her chair, dangling her slippers from her bare feet, crumbling a sugared tamarind between her fingers – as the woman I had known back in Soekaboemi and afterwards in Batavia. And why she was living with Abdullah's relatives was a mystery to me. There was no shortage of accommodation in Soerabaja, so there must surely have been alternative ways to remain close to Oeroeg.

Among the old-fashioned furniture on the veranda stood a variety of cages containing twittering and fluttering birds. A mynah bird sat tied to its perch by a thin chain. Here too there were rows of ferns and various plants in ornamental china pots. The back garden was shaded, almost entirely overarched by the boughs and trailing air roots of a *waringin* tree. I know it sounds strange, but for a moment I had the sensation that there was some link between this shadowy back veranda, with all its plants and birds, and Telaga Hideung – the way I had last seen it when a cloud passed over the sun. That sensation was only partly dispelled when one of Abdullah's cousins lit an oil lamp in a globe of frosted glass, which was promptly swarming with insects.

After the evening meal the talk became a little more animated. Lida told me about her job at the hospital, in a new drawling tone of voice that I found unsettling.

I asked her why she was not working in a European hospital. She exchanged looks with Oeroeg and Abdullah, the meaning of which eluded me entirely.

'She speaks Malay very well these days,' said Oeroeg. 'And she's also learning Javanese.'

'So I can help when Oeroeg starts working among the native population,' Lida added, without taking her eyes off her foster son.

'Later on . . . it'll come in handy,' said Oeroeg, with the flicker of a smile.

'You'll be working for the government, I take it,' I said, not so much to hear him confirm this as to steer the conversation back to a topic I could follow.

Abdullah, who was shelling peanuts, brought his head up sharply.

'No, I won't be working for the government,' Oeroeg said.

'But I thought you were getting a grant from them,' I ventured.

'She's the one who's paying for my studies,' said Oeroeg, inclining his head towards Lida.

I looked from the one to the other. Insects whirred and buzzed around the lamp. The old man, who had little to say, rocked silently back and forth in his chair, while

Lida fiddled with a bamboo splinter in the edge of the table. But both Oeroeg and Abdullah met my gaze. Suddenly I felt that this was a moment they had long been anticipating. They wanted to challenge their adversary. To them, at that stage, I was the symbol, the personification, of something they had turned against with all their being. I struggled to hold on to a sense of reality, which was fast threatening to escape me on this quiet back veranda.

'Well, what does that mean then?' I asked Oeroeg.

'That I don't fancy taking handouts from the government,' he replied evenly. 'I don't need your help.'

'Our help?' I said, the blood rushing to my head as the meaning of his words sank in. 'Oh, so you don't mind accepting Lida's help?'

'Lida thinks the same way as we do,' Oeroeg said proudly.

One thing led to another, and ultimately to a discussion during which I was kept on the defensive due to sheer ignorance on my part. I knew next to nothing about the upsurge of nationalist sentiment, the unofficial schools that were being set up, the ferment of unrest in certain sections of native society. I listened in silence as Oeroeg and Abdullah, all aflame, railed against the injustices of

the colonial government, against the Dutch and against
white people in general. Much of what they said struck
me as unfounded or exaggerated, but I was at a loss for
counter arguments. My astonishment grew by the minute:
in his new milieu of radical students and young agitators
Oeroeg had turned into an orator.

'The *desa* folk, the common people, have been kept
dumb for a purpose,' he said vehemently, looking straight
at me as he leaned forward across the table. 'It was in
your interest to prevent them from developing. But those
days are over. We'll see to that. They don't need *wayang*
puppets or *gamelans*, and none of those superstitions
or *doekoens* either – we're not living in the empire of
Mataram any more, nor is there any reason why Java
should look like a postcard for tourists. All that stuff
is just ballast. The temple at Boroboedoer is nothing but
a heap of old stones. Let them give us factories, and
warships and modern clinics and schools, and a say in our
own affairs . . .'

As Oeroeg held forth, raising his fist for emphasis, I
registered the staring faces of the others as in a dream.
In a dusky corner of the back veranda, outside the pool
of lamplight, Abdullah's cousins were whispering among
themselves. The old man kept nodding his head approv-

ingly. Abdullah carried on shelling peanuts throughout, but when he looked up, I saw his eyes glinting behind his glasses.

Lida murmured, 'Yes, yes indeed,' at regular intervals. She had lifted the bamboo splinter from the table, and was now busy splicing it into thin fibres with her fingernail. Not once did she look at me. I had the feeling that she was slightly discomfited by my presence, that she knew in the depths of her being that this new ideal was a last resort for her lonely, childlike heart. I was overcome with sympathy for her. Had I been able to conceive of all these things more rationally at the time, the conversation might have taken a different turn. As it was I sat there facing Oeroeg and Abdullah, feeling as if I were part of a bad dream.

This sense of unreality persisted even when I went to bed in the guest room that had been prepared for me. Through the wide-open windows I saw the stars twinkling beyond the branches of the *waringin* tree. All around me were the manifold whispers of the East Indies night so familiar to my ear, and yet, in some peculiar way, I felt an outsider. From the next room came the hushed voices of Oeroeg and Abdullah. The division between their world and mine was complete.

I left for Europe. There is no need to dwell here on the ensuing period: my brief stay with my mother in Nice and my student years in Delft, which were interrupted by the outbreak of war and then broken off entirely due to restrictions imposed by the Germans. I was modestly active in the resistance, like most people I knew. I became increasingly preoccupied with thoughts of Oeroeg and Lida, of my father and his family, at whose fate I could only guess. After the capitulation of Japan I began to receive a trickle of news. I learned that my father was dead, and that Eugenie and the children were in Batavia waiting for transportation to Holland. About Oeroeg and Lida I heard nothing at all, despite my repeated efforts to trace them. I completed my studies and then did what I had been planning to do for years: I applied for a job in the Indies. The chaotic situation there in the aftermath of the Japanese occupation did not worry me unduly. The troubles would be only temporary, I was sure. The 'colonial' way of thinking so often criticised – rightly or wrongly – in post-war Holland was not something I identified with. My wish to return to the Indies and work there arose primarily from a deep-seated sense of commitment to the country where I had been born and brought up. The years in Holland, important as they had been, counted for less than my childhood and schooldays over there.

If it is true that there is a landscape of the soul for each one of us – a certain atmosphere, an image that strikes a chord in the furthest reaches of our being – then my personal landscape was – and is – the mountain slopes of the Preanger: the bitter fragrance of tea bushes, the splash of clear streams coursing over rocks, the blue shadows of clouds moving across the plains. That my yearning for all this could be crippling was something I had experienced in the war years, when deprived of every contact or hope of return. Nor was my enthusiasm dampened when I met Eugenie in The Hague and heard her raging hysterically against the land of horrors she had left behind.

My arrival in Batavia coincided with the start of what I will call, for the sake of simplicity, the 'police actions'*, undertaken by the Dutch military. I found no trace of Oeroeg. There was no information on the fate of the

* Translator's note: police actions (*politionele acties*) was the euphemistic term used by the Dutch government for its military offensives against participants in the Indonesian struggle for independence.

medical students of those days. Wandering the streets of Batavia, shabbier now but still recognizable, the way a familiar face marked by suffering and age remains identifiable, I automatically scanned the crowds for Oeroeg. A hundred times I thought I saw him, and equally often I was disappointed. One day I spotted Abdullah in a jostling crowd in front of the ANETA Press Agency where a communiqué was being issued. I recognised him immediately by his glasses, although he looked dishevelled and much thinner than before. 'Abdullah!' I cried, over the sea of heads separating us. He craned his neck and looked about him. Did he see me? The sunlight glittered on his glasses, so I could not see his eyes. He paused a moment, facing towards me. I wanted to go up to him, but when I was a few metres away he passed me, moving in the opposite direction. I called out to him again, pushing people aside in my agitation, but Abdullah had vanished into the throng.

I was assigned to work on the reconstruction of bridges destroyed by the republicans in the Preanger. My first posting was only a few hours' drive from Kebon Djati, and as soon as the opportunity arose I could not resist joining an inspection patrol heading in that direction. I stood in the open army truck, gazing out over the beloved landscape. On either side of the rutted, pot-holed road were the same green foothills, the same bamboo thickets I remembered from the old days. The flooded *sawahs* glittered in the sunshine, mirroring not only the clouds drifting across the sky in unchanged tranquillity, but also telegraph poles, leaning sideways or cut down and tangled up with broken cables. Straggles of people in filthy rags stared blankly after the truck. Only the shrill voices of the small children jumping up and down on the side of the road could be heard above the rumble of the wheels. All that remained of the station where Oeroeg and I used to catch the train to Soekaboemi was an outline of blackened stones. Weeds and bushes had sprung up where the food stalls once stood, and the *desa* dwellings across the way had disappeared.

We came to a bend in the road, and I knew we had reached the outskirts of the tea gardens, from where, in the old days, you could just glimpse the manager's house further up on the slope, a smudge of white among the endless rows of bushes. I leaned out over the side of the truck, my heart in my throat. I knew better than to expect it to fit my mental image of the place, and to have survived unscathed, given that Kebon Djati had lain in the path of the retreating republicans. But however unkempt and weed-infested the plantation might be, this was my homecoming.

The landscape rolling out before me at the bend in the road was unlike anything I had imagined, even in my worst nightmares. The scorched hilltops were eerily bare. The truck drove up the road as though between the ribs of a giant cadaver. At one point I thought I had missed the house, and at the same instant realised that it was no longer there. I could barely tell where it had once stood. The driver suggested driving up to the ruins to take a look – the patrol had been there before to take stock of the damage. But I declined the offer and we kept to the main road leading into the black hills.

Not until we entered the tunnel of forest did I find myself in surroundings that matched the memory stored in my brain. The same ice-cold streams trickled down the steep, fern-carpeted slopes, the same smell of earth and decaying vegetation wafted towards us from the shadowy depths of green. I recognised what was surely the place where the footpath to Telaga Hideung was hidden in the brushwood, and asked the others if we could stop for a moment. They were happy to comply, and jumped down from the truck to stretch their legs.

I made an excuse and slipped away into the trees.

I walked quickly, even though the path was barely recog-
nisable under the dense growth. I kept my sights on the
treetops, and on the shimmer of light in the leafy distance,
where I knew the sunlight streamed down to the lake
through the ravine. Birds whose names I had forgotten
sang all around me, unseen among the leaves. The air was
filled with the same constant mysterious rustling sound
that will forever mark that jungle in my mind. The lake
too, black and shining, the water plants and the faint
breeze making ripples on the surface – I found them all
unchanged. A wood pigeon called with sweet insistence
from the dark trees across the lake. I squatted down by
the water's edge and gazed at the treetops flaring golden-
green in the upper reaches of the ravine as they caught the
sun. No sound came from the water, and only the occasional slithering of a toad or a lizard could be heard
among the overhanging plants. The aerial roots of the
trees appeared to float motionless on the surface of the
water. The wood pigeon repeated its call, now from close
by, it seemed. It made me think of Oeroeg and me in our
striped playsuits, perched on the steps of the back veranda
at Kebon Djati while the pigeons cooed endlessly in their
cages behind the servants' quarters.

The grasses on the bank whispered in the breeze, and

again there were ripples on the water. I thought I saw the reddish shimmer in the deep, like dark blood, that I remembered from all those years ago. That same image had come to me on the back veranda at Abdullah's – why?

A shadow fell on the ground beside me. I looked up and saw a slight, swarthy figure in dirty khaki shorts with a batik head-cloth wound casually round his tousled hair. He stared at me with a fierce yet unseeing gaze, and motioned with his revolver that I should raise my arms. 'Oeroeg!' I said, half-aloud. The wood pigeon flew up from its tree with a clatter of wings.

How long we stood facing each other in silence I do not know. I made no movement, neither did he. I waited, but without any sense of fear or tension, in complete calm. It occurred to me that this moment was the inescapable culmination of all that had gone before, from the time Oeroeg and I were born. It had grown in us and ripened, though not of our own will or consciousness. Here for the first time we were at a point where we each faced the other in all truthfulness.

He levelled his gun.

'I'm not alone,' I said, although I do not believe that it was fear making me say this. I truly did not care whether he shot me or not.

The expression on his face remained impassive, but he released his index finger from the trigger, from which I concluded that he, unlike me, was on his own.

'Go away,' he said in Soendanese. 'Go away, or I'll shoot. You have no business being here.'

I saw that he had grown pale. A scar on his cheek stood out more sharply than before. 'Listen,' I began, but he interrupted me angrily: 'Go away. Mind your own business.' His eyes glittered darkly like the surface of Telaga Hideung, with the same refusal to reveal what lay submerged in the deep.

I could see it was madness to think of engaging him in conversation. All he was prepared to reveal was there before my eyes. Tied round his right arm was a grimy strip of cloth on which I could make out a red cross. The Javanese dagger in his belt, the head-cloth folded in the Soendanese way, the American-style khaki shorts, the revolver – perhaps left-over from the Japanese occupation – all these things spoke of the stages he had passed through.

'Go away,' he repeated.

I twisted round to look at Telaga Hideung: ancient crater transformed into a lake by the rain, mirror of trees and clouds, playground of light and shade, of the breeze and the water-snake, the secret domain that betrayed its impersonal cruelty in the shimmer of blood and the grasping stems beneath the black surface.

A cloud passed over the sun, and the lake gleamed coldly, like ink and lead. The shrill tones of a patrol whistle sounded from afar. A signal to me. His eyes darted like lightning around the forest. He was no longer thinking of me. Every muscle in his body was strained for defence, for flight. He stood half-turned away from me, in deliberation with himself. The tendons in his neck and his bony shoulder blades were visible through the tears in his shirt. He was at once pitiful and terrifying: there was a look of hunted prey, but also the calculating intelligence that had destroyed *desas* and burned the hills to black. One more moment I saw him standing there against the dark backdrop of jungle. Voices from the patrol could be heard close by, on the path between the trees. I looked again, but he had already vanished, in which direction I could not tell. The leaves barely stirred, it could have been the wind. I walked back and rejoined the patrol. Had it really been Oeroeg? I do not know, and never will. I have even lost the ability to recognise him.

My only purpose here has been to write an account of our shared youth. I wanted to preserve an image of those years before they pass into oblivion like a wisp of smoke in the wind. Kebon Djati is a memory, and so is the school boarding-house, and Lida; Abdullah and I cross paths without a word, and I will never meet Oeroeg again. I do not pretend to have understood him. I knew him, just as I knew Telaga Hideung, as a reflecting surface – I never fathomed the depths. Is it too late? Am I forever to be a stranger in the land of my birth, to the soil from which I am loath to be uprooted? Time will tell.

Glossary

Note: the old Dutch spelling of place names and vernacular words has been retained. As there was no standard spelling of the strain of Malay spoken in the East Indies at the time, the Dutch devised their own spelling. One of the main differences is 'oe'– pronounced 'oo' in Dutch – which has been replaced in modern Indonesian by 'u'.

baboe – female domestic servant, nursemaid
bami – noodles
Batavia – colonial name of present-day Jakarta
branie – flaunting, swaggering behaviour
desa – independent hamlet
djongos – houseboy
doekoen – herbalist, medicine man
gamelan – Javanese orchestra, mainly percussion
goelali – candy sugar

Indo – Eurasian

kampong – generally: native settlement within a city, but also: the collection of worker's dwellings on an estate

katjang – peanut, common term of disparagement for mixed race

ketan – sticky-rice sweetmeat

klontong – Chinese door-to-door vendor of small wares

mandoer – overseer, foreman

pasar – market

pikolan – pole carried over the shoulder with a load at either end.

potong – to cut, operate on

rijsttafel – 'rice-table', elaborate meal with a multitude of dishes

sawah – irrigated rice field

sinjo besar – big master

slendang – rectangle of cloth worn over the shoulder or used to carry babies or objects

Soendanese – language of western Java, spoken in the historical region of Soenda

tambleang – *Lantana camara*, species of verbena

trasih – fish paste

waringin – Ficus, banyan tree, venerated in Java

wayang – shadow theatre